Dear

In

a

Van

Aug 28 2013

THE TIME MERCHANTS

and other strange tales

THE TIME MERCHANTS

and other strange tales

Vasudev Murthy

LiFi Publications Pvt. Ltd.
New Delhi

Published by:
LiFi Publications Pvt. Ltd.
211, 2nd Floor, Gagandeep
12, Rajendra Place, New Delhi - 110 008, India
Phone : (011) 2574 1000
E-mail : info@lifipublications.com
Web : www.lifipublications.com

ISBN 13: 978-93-82536-07-9 ISBN 10: 93-82536-07-8

First published in 2013

Cataloging in Publication Data—DK
[Courtesy: D.K. Agencies (P) Ltd. <docinfo@dkagencies.com>]

Murthy, Vasudev.
The time merchants and other strange tales / Vasudev Murthy.
p. cm.
Short stories.
ISBN 9789382536079

1. Fantasy fiction, Indic (English) 2. Short stories, Indic (English). I. Title.

DDC 823.92 23

Printed in India by D.K. Fine Art Press (P) Ltd., Delhi - 52

To

Amogha and Sarang

Some stories can be written. Some cannot.

With Love

Your Father

Contents

Foreword

Vasudev Murthy's stories are those of a lulling, gentle, whimsical and unobtrusive fantasy. It is a distinct voice that does not merely rehearse the many familiar conflicts that Indian writers in English are sanctioned to depict—urbanization, diaspora, new forms of emergent sexuality. Rather, it opens the window to wider possibilities of plot and imagination. This ought to be where we should invest the best of our future writing—the articulation of the new, as well as the inventiveness in depicting, and remaking alive, the over-familiar, the seemingly-mundane.

The form of the fragment is married to a form of science fiction. What is opened is a quirky window into the metaphysical—the trick here is not to be heavy-handed, but only to suggest. What could be more weighty topics than the Time and human greed and finitude and spiritual cannibalism depicted in the first story? And yet the touch is redeemingly, crucially, light. This makes the 'elixir' (as the story would have it) more unfailingly potent. So too, the mysterious forces that bring a pure mathematician and a Sanskrit scholar together in *The Mathematician.* It is Murthy's wit that saves and sharpens the situation (the equations that hover in the air, the disappearance of the laughing scholars as they leave a trail of jasmine), and makes the story itself a perfumed sliver of droll humor.

Other stories of Vasudev Murthy continue his long standing, and deeply informed engagement with music, especially Hindustani classical music—he is a practitioner who has performed with many distinguished classical musicians. In *The Tanpura,* he continues the delicate anthropomorphization of music that he had achieved so deftly in his earlier work, *What the Raags told me.* The story that follows in the collection—*The Madness of Music,* persists with the music theme: here music soaks and saturates a life from the very moment of birth. Is genius ever anything but a curse, a burden that is bound to doom one? Is death to be the only joyous redemption? Yet the touch of the story is again light, and the growing and passing of a whole life is depicted so completely and satisfyingly in a few pages. Such a story passes beyond the confines of those easily recognized as tragic or redemptive, or of lives easily recognized as successful or failed.

The wide variety of themes, contexts and characters testifies to the great ambition of a book that is actually not so large—a hundred and sixty or so pages. Yet the book, though written so niftily, is not so easy to read. One can't race through them in a quick sitting—or maybe one can, but one shouldn't. Rather, they should be savored slowly, and one should let the distilled experience bleed into one's consciousness. Perhaps one story for each of the lazy, leisured afternoons that one can smuggle from the week or month. Perhaps they should be read many times, once fast and once (or more times) at a slow and lenient pace, so that they may satiate better with the full force of their control that Vasudev Murthy so often (and seemingly so easily) manages.

Prof. Nikhil Govind
(Ph.D., University of California at Berkeley)
Centre for Philosophy and Humanities
Manipal University

1

The Time Merchants

They resisted. The struggle was hard to witness even for one so inured to it as myself, a Time Merchant.

But practically everyone and everything was in our net. Whatever lived did so on our terms. They bought Time from us again and again, convinced that on *this* occasion, they would be successful in living forever and cheating us. It had never yet worked, but the temptation was always too intense.

And so they were born. Again and again. As men and women. They bought Time from us and started the journey. In the beginning, they were cocky and confident with the brashness of infancy and youth. Death seemed distant and not even a possibility. Their parents died and so did their friends. But *they* felt they wouldn't and they were sure about it. They exercised, dieted and prayed. They did whatever it took to develop resistance to death. And they always forgot that they had bought Time from us.

So they struggled. Every now and then, we would send them reminders that Time, that which they had bought, was ticking away. It was in different forms – a sickness here, a dream there. Resistance was futile. But what do you do when the desire to live forever is so overpowering that it walks over reason?

Finally, it would come. The last strand of allocated Time, the last grain, was consumed. Like moths fighting against the lure of light, they fought hard. But there was no way at all that they could be successful. Inexorable. They would finally sink in the quicksand of Existence.

And always, they left their bodies convinced at the last moment that now they had understood the trick of perpetual existence, and when they had to apply it. And so they came again. Planning to cheat us.

It was such opium! Fifty, sixty, seventy, eighty years of existence and it was never enough! They wanted more! And more!

They rushed to the Marketplace demanding more Time. And we sold them some more. We were merchants. What did we care? If there was demand, and there was supply, why did we have to question the very need for the commodity? Who were we to apply moral constructs to the matter?

You ask – how did they pay for it? Why, with Time of course! It really was a loan of a kind. Each was given an amount of time by the Order when they were formed. They were allowed to trade it for an existence of their choice. Our price was a small percentage. So if they were given Eighty Units, we would keep one and give them seventy-nine back in the form that they wanted. When they came back and wanted more, they would have to part with one more and get a new life for seventy-eight. And so on. It was quite simple actually. Do you understand?

Obviously, at some point it would dry up completely. They became more and more desperate each time they returned. They loved the experiences so much that they had to have more – but they received less and less! We couldn't be emotional about these things.

It was horrible to see them return after having lived as babies for only a year and wanting to go back. Even that experience had been intoxicating. They wanted to again feel the softness of their mothers and the rough affection of their fathers. They wanted that cozy cradle and deluge of love from everyone else. We could understand. But we couldn't help. Business is business. If you want to go back and live for a single day, that was your business – you just had to pay for it.

You say we were cruel? I'm sorry you feel that way. But we really couldn't do anything about it. We had no powers to advise them. And so we were reduced to watching their antics and droll lives and how they went about grandly imposing upon themselves a feeling of importance and permanence. Some seemed to understand the silliness of the whole thing but even they, when the moment came, did not want to leave. But they did.

And after the journey they came to us again. We avoided comment. Merchants must have tact.

What did we do with the Time we collected as fees? Well, we liquefied it and drank it every now and then. That was our elixir and it helped us truly live forever. Not that we thought gravely about such issues. It was an amusing business, if you thought about it.

But we had collected so much Time that we had to put it to other uses.

So we bargained with the Order (You call it 'God' or something, don't you? How quaint!) And expanded our business into other dimensions. Please do contact us. I'm sure we can help you – for a price, of course.

2

The Web

I sit silently and upright on the chair placed in the middle of an otherwise empty room. At my feet are my drawings and I look at them intently. There is no one else in the room. Straight ahead is the door through which I know people peer in to look at me curiously. Yes, I cannot see them from my side, but I can sense them. It makes no difference and I pity them that they have so little to do that they find looking at me a source of excitement.

So I am a psychiatric case and not normal. Indeed. And is everyone else normal?

What does normal mean anyway? Who can be called normal? You, perhaps? You who claim to function within the parameters of normally accepted behaviour? So your brain chemistry is fine and mine is not. My congratulations!

I was put in here because I believe I was always lost in thought and sat absolutely silently, never responding to anyone. They use words like 'catatonic' and 'stupor'. I have been brought here because people do not like those who sit quietly minding their own business, not seeking any kind of stimulation or social contact. I have heard them whisper that my case is unusual because I am not violent, do not talk to myself or to imaginary friends, and have actually not had any serious incident happen that might have pushed me over the brink. In other words, I have apparently not experienced any wrenching trauma. The only thing I do is sit and draw webs. Spider webs – where the spiders are always missing.

In fact, they are right. I really haven't had anything bad happen. Nothing like the death of a child or a complete collapse of my marriage or loss of a job or anything sensational. What actually happened was that I developed an interest in spider webs. That obsession for spider webs then led me to the edge of an astounding discovery, which I simply cannot tell anyone about till I know for sure, myself.

One Sunday afternoon, I sat on the lawn behind my house right next to a tree, enjoying the sun's warmth. Quite by chance, I saw a web at the base of the tree trunk near some roots that were partially exposed. I turned to my side and propped myself up with my elbow, supporting my head with the palm of my left hand. I studied the web closely; something drew me to it.

The centre was difficult to focus on. Clear, definite hexagons spread out one after the other, each larger than the other. They swayed gently but otherwise shimmered whenever a fleck of light fell on them.

Somehow, the feeling came into my mind that this was not just any old conventional web. There was more to it. I looked around and saw several more in the neighbourhood. Beautiful cascading perfect hexagons inviting insects to visit.

But wait – that was it! None of the webs had any prey stuck and desiccated in them. They were clean – and not because they were new. And there were no spiders in the vicinity that I could detect.

I ran inside and brought out my drawing sheets and some pencils and an eraser. I tried to draw a few but could not capture their beauty well enough. It's very difficult to draw white lines on white paper. To draw in black would be unjust. To the web.

I went elsewhere in the garden and found plenty of webs. None of them had any distinct repeated geometry. They were classic ones with gossamer silk with dead prey hopelessly stuck in them. They had lost. The spider had won.

At about this time, a little nerve from deep within my brain stretching to a point on my back seemed to come alive. It is there even today, a mild distinct tingle, an electric movement. I mention this only for the sake of completeness. I became aware of it and the webs at about the same time. It was as though I had developed a first strand within myself – yes, that sounds ridiculous.

Every day in the afternoon, I went back to the base of the tree and looked for those webs again. Yes, they were expanding. I felt I simply had to document them and so kept sketching them. I searched for a spider but could never find one. I even looked with a magnifying glass, but it was of no use. Day after day, this drama continued – sterile webs expanding apparently by themselves, and me sketching them. I have carefully documented them over a period of six years without skipping a day, as you have doubtlessly been informed.

All of a sudden, I saw something in one web, after six long years of relentless study. It seemed like a very unusual insect. It was red and vaguely cylindrical – almost like a little red bullet – and was moving about freely; apparently the strands were not sticky. That was puzzling. It moved in a peculiar sideways manner, rapidly from end to end, stopped periodically and then started again. I was astounded.

The next day, I could hardly wait to go back and see what the web looked like.

Several extraordinary events had taken place. For one, the very colour of the webs had changed – they were now a distinct deep blue. For another, those bugs had multiplied and were moving about rapidly with a purpose. And finally, the hexagon had become a pentagon.

How had entire structures rebuilt or rather remodeled themselves overnight? I continued my sketching and drawing, my fingers trembling a bit. I had to rush inside and get coloring pencils. My mother looked at me wearily. She had stopped asking about my hobby a long time ago.

I started fantasizing about these webs all through the day and night. I could barely sleep, wondering what would happen the next morning. But nothing happened at all.

For the next two years, nothing changed and my pile of sketches reached the ceiling. I knew something very important was imminent but I did not want to share it with anyone. My heart would pound whenever I recalled those two events. I could not understand why no one else had seen them.

And then again, it happened. One fine day, the pentagons had become transformed into perfect squares! And the blue became a blood red! I assure you, I did not imagine it. It really happened. The day before it was a set of perfectly symmetrical blue pentagons and now they were a set of perfect red squares. And the bugs had suddenly become perfectly circular bright yellow discs moving about in precise straight lines.

I shivered with excitement. And as you will note from my album of sketches, these changes have been documented.

Now I could sense them talking to me. They asked me questions. What was my name? What species was I? Why was I interested in them? They conveyed their appreciation for the fact that I had neither destroyed their webs nor captured any of them.

I understood quite soon – I am quite an intelligent person Sir, though the men in white robes might claim otherwise – that these fantastic beings were not insects at all. They had an amazing amount of collective intelligence and a *plan*. I tried asking but the only answer I could get was: study your sketches very closely and the answer will become obvious.

And so I have been studying my sketches very, very carefully. The problem is, of course, that I have over five thousand sketches, and while each is distinct, it is very difficult for me to comprehend and keep track of the subtle differences that I detect. I need peace and quiet and cannot be disturbed. It is like putting together a huge jigsaw puzzle, but not quite like that either. This is very difficult to explain.

But I have been able to deduce a few important facts. The purpose of these webs is anything but mild or benign. There is a greater plan, a greater purpose. But with nothing really to show to anyone, it is impossible to get anyone's attention. I do know that the next transformation of these webs will be perfect circles and then they will expand into the third dimension. Does that mean layers of circular webs? Are we talking of an acceleration in their expansion? Does this mean that we will suddenly be confronted by expanding steel cylinders crisscrossing our path? Would that not worry you?

I tried to share this with my mother who reluctantly followed me to the garden. But the webs were gone! My mother shook her head and returned. I felt cheated.

But when I returned to the spot, the webs were back! They did not want my mother to see them, clearly.

In any case, my mother has brought me here. She is convinced that I have gone mad. I can hardly blame her. Had I been in her position, I would certainly feel the same. However, since I have not harmed anyone in any manner, why should you hold me? Long hours of silent observation and studying my sketches have rendered me almost mute. I do not feel like saying anything. But I request you to release me. I must go back to the garden and pick up where I was interrupted. I can feel it in my bones that something lethal is going to be unleashed and I want to be ready to warn everyone about it.

Thank you for your attention.

3

Strange Memories

My memory is not what it used to be. Or what it should be. I get things mixed up. My sense of *deja vu* is acute one moment. The next moment I am unable to recall anything about surroundings and people that I am very familiar with.

And yet I live a perfectly normal life. I have a job. I live with someone who says she is my wife. I live with two children who seem fond of me and call me 'Papa'. We are comfortable, I believe, and even have a small car. We have a nice house.

I guess all this is good.

I use the company bus to go to work. I have been doing this for years. Everything is predictable – the people who climb on, the distances, the road, the sights along the way. I seem to know every stone on the pavement across the road. I know how the houses that we pass by look like – I mean, I know what to expect exactly. The colour, the design, and the people who are likely to come out or go in at about the time my bus passes by. I know the handle bar I clutch for balance very well as I sit in my seat in the bus. When I grip it, I feel safe, because I have been doing that for years.

And yet I have always remained disconnected.

One part of me – I shall call it the visible part – interacts with the environment automatically and correctly. I say all the right things. I smile on cue. I am silent when necessary. My conversations seem smooth and normal. I understand that I come across as intelligent and well-informed. I am a well-integrated anonymous member of society.

The other part – I shall call it the invisible part – watches all this passively. This is apparently the real me. I do not advise the visible part. I do not influence it. I am not influenced by it either. This, the real me, as it were, merely observes, though it does not record. Yes, all this is quite confusing, and yet it probably makes sense.

This has been going on since as far back as I can recall.

But every now and then, something comes out from this invisible part. Something unexpected. Something peculiar. It appears to be a strand of memory from some other time or place. It might be of me travelling in a train in Japan. It might be of me reading a book at twilight in a small hut in a remote part of the Andes Mountains. It might be of me in the midst of a perfectly normal boisterous family get-together in a town in Spain, where the people are well known to me and everything meshes together effortlessly. Or it might be of me as a policeman walking in the afternoon in a market in Thailand, saying hello to all the people who I have known for years along that beat. The smells, the colours, and the feel of the air, the odours, and the languages – all of them are perfectly recognizable and part of that reality.

In the normal course, this has never disturbed me. Naturally, I have always believed that these things happen to everyone. I cannot say that this is not true since I have not peeped into the minds of anyone else. These unexpected memories crept into my consciousness while I was doing something entirely different, but it never really bothered me. Why? Because they were infrequent and their 'intrusion' was as gentle as their departure. I felt a mild sense of pleasure when I experienced them and was always able to shrug them away if they interrupted my attention to other matters.

But recently, the ease with which I handled these dichotomous planes has eroded.

The invisible part has become more restive. Assertive would be a better word. It is no longer content to simply remain idle and ejaculate something harmless from time to time. It now demands my attention. Whatever it says is a little stronger, a little more pungent and a little less easy to shrug away.

For instance, during one of my bus rides to work, as I watched the traffic outside with my normal glazed indifference, I suddenly felt myself actually being murdered. The scene was vivid. I was somewhere in Africa. I was saying something very heated to two or three men. It was dark and hot. Knives were flashed. I took one out myself. Though I was able to keep one of them away and even inflicted a scratch on his cheek as I made a feint, one other came in from the side and jammed a knife in my ribs. I felt a sharp agonizing pain and felt the stainless cold steel sliding through my muscle. I felt the blood gushing out. I heard myself screaming with pain and then felt a greater darkness and an ink-black night as I actually died.

I do not know if I actually said anything. As I was pulled back to my existence in the bus, I found that I was clutching the handlebar very tightly. I stole a look around me. No one had noticed anything. Everyone was busy doing the very same things they had done for all the years I had known them to do at exactly that moment in the morning on my way to work. Someone reading a newspaper, someone else a magazine, someone, more taciturn, absorbed in his own thoughts…

I was puzzled by the violence of this memory. It was excessively real. I looked inwards to see my invisible part doing exactly what I had seen it do ninety-nine percent of the time – absolutely nothing. But I detected a hint of something sly. Yes, it wasn't an accident. It was mischief. And it wasn't funny at all. But of course, there was nothing I could do about it.

That very day, as I was absorbed in investigating a line item in a ledger (did I tell you I am an accountant by profession?), I saw the numbers dance. The numbers across the entire page (which was on the right) undulated gently, almost as if they were on the surface of a still lake that had been disturbed by the falling of a pebble in the center. The page on the left was exactly as it had always been – lifeless, entirely neutral, without any opinion.

I suddenly felt myself diving deep into that shimmering page. I was being pulled in by something and I was holding my breath. My eyes were wide open and the light at the surface lessened as I went deeper and deeper into the water.

There was absolutely nothing I was being allowed to do. My limbs were paralyzed. Though my lungs shrieked with pain, I could neither exhale nor inhale – not that I didn't want to. I simply could *not*. I never knew what happened but I was being eaten by *something* and that entire memory was preserved. Sharp teeth shredded me like cabbage, my bones were crushed – it was extremely vivid. But fear completely neutralized the pain I was feeling. And then there was a *blank*.

This time, as I came back to reality, I found myself literally gasping for breath and sprawling on the chair. Miraculously, no one had noticed again, simply because there was no one around who might have.

Looking inward again, I saw my invisible part. This time, it was glowing even more. It almost looked back at me with some defiance. There was a hint of a challenge.

Was I dealing with my own memories from past births? Or was I actually being a kind of voyeur, participating actively in someone else's memories? Had this invisible part of me hijacked floating wisps of memories of diverse individuals and "loaded" them on me?

I prepared myself for further assaults. And that was just as it should have been. Because the intrusions became more frequent, more challenging, more vivid. It was all I could do to keep a thin line between reality and this grim random documentary that kept trying to steal my balance. Someone or something was trying to swap my reality with something else. I might not have minded it so much if these completely random strands of memories were occasionally peaceful, benign and pleasant. But no; all were excessively violent and disturbing.

Somehow, I have grappled with this problem and managed to keep myself away from appearing insane. If I go to a psychiatrist, he would undoubtedly suggest rest and relaxation accompanied by several drugs. "Brain chemistry imbalance. Slightly schizophrenic. Nothing to be alarmed about. Happens all the time," he might say blandly. I know from age and experience that it is a mistake to try to explain events in the recesses of one's brains to others, in the hope that they would understand. Everyone has his or her own personal hell. Each is skeptical about the validity of anyone else's mental gymnastics. It is better to be silent and live in a balance with the torment within and carry on with the routine.

But whether the invisible part of me will allow me to control it thus is another matter. It seems to be able to grab the ethereal wisps of extremely grim memories of people long gone and present it to me and chortle. Does it feel thwarted by my ability to control it or at least contain its effect? And will it suddenly grab and present something so incredibly warped and demented that I will clutch my hair with both hands and scream with agony and start a chain of events that will see me in an asylum, protesting to the weary guard that I'm just fine?

4

The Mathematician

I am a Professor of Mathematics at a college in a small town lost somewhere in the depths of India, affiliated to a very ordinary University about 150 kilometers away. The college produces a small stream of Arts and Science Graduates, none of whom possess ambition or skill. I am myself quite mediocre and most students probably forget me the moment they complete their tedious three years and leave town seeking better prospects in the larger cities. I do not teach well and I do not enjoy it either. No one cares. For me, it is a job. I have long since reconciled with my ordinariness and do not get any rush of excitement from preparing for my class. I do not research; it is not required. Where once, in my youth, I tingled with excitement when I solved difficult differential equations, I now wonder what the fuss is all about.

But it is not I that I write about, but my former colleague, Dr. Sawhney.

In this sea of ordinariness – we were six Professors with PhDs from mediocre Universities – Dr. Sawhney stood out. He took ten years to complete his Doctorate in a very esoteric area of Pure Mathematics that no one cared about and so was a little older than I, though he joined my Department two years after me. The rest of us immediately realized that he was a genius, but all, without exception, did not resent his brilliance, because we knew that he too would disappear into nothingness and anonymity like we had. Who cared about brilliant mathematicians in a dusty town in the middle of nowhere?

We watched his predictable frantic attempts to attract research grants with mild amusement because we knew he would never succeed. We were right. Welcome to the real world. He did not have contacts and he actually believed that merit was all that mattered. And, as reality hit, he became bitter too like us.

But there was a difference.

His brilliance actually increased as his hatred for the 'establishment' increased. His lectures were extraordinarily – *frighteningly* – different. Everything in the syllabus that needed to be covered, he covered. But he always added a little something, which was considered 'out of the syllabus'. His examples hinted of the connection between Mathematics and the darker side of the spiritual world.

His eyes sparkled with raw energy; he paced the podium like a man possessed and his voice ranged in whispers to sheer screams, as he described the power of simple algebraic equations and their actual meaning in a different dimension.

There was always absolute silence. At various times, when we felt inclined, we attended his lectures, as did the Principal. We could find no flaw in his style or the content. He taught what was supposed to be taught. His students did well enough. No complaint could be brought against him. So we let him continue as an oddity in an otherwise completely bland environment. Moreover, he was quite nice to us and would always be glad to stand in for us whenever we didn't feel like lecturing.

His best friend was a Professor Shastri, a short and inconspicuous Sanskrit scholar. He was a transplant from South India and was, on the whole, quite like us. He knew where he stood; he knew there was no future in teaching Sanskrit, but also knew his Government job was safe, student or no student. This allowed him to do his private research into old Sanskrit texts.

Prof. Shastri and Prof. Sawhney spent hours together discussing their findings. They were clearly influenced by each other and they must have exchanged thoughts and ideas. Dr. Sawhney's lectures would make abrupt references to Sanskrit texts and *shlokas*, which he claimed had mathematical undertones and contained hints of a different darker plane of reality. Examples in Matrices, Differential Equations, Numerical Analysis, Logic and Fluid Dynamics would touch upon a bridge somewhere to the nether world. The average student would find the analogues and veiled references puzzling, but a brighter one would find these examples an inflection point, where his mild curiosity would turn into a serious interest and a determination to master the area. Now how could anyone fault that?

One summer, Prof. Shastri and Prof. Sawhney went away together on a vacation to the Himalayas. Being bachelors, they could do precisely what they wanted. I heard later from Prof. Sawhney, that they had traveled beyond Devprayag and Rudraprayag to the hamlet of Shivgaon, tucked in the folds of a difficult-to-reach valley beyond the snow line.

When they returned, they were different. Uncannily different. Their eyes burned. The air pulsed about them. They walked menacingly. They did not talk, they snarled. These were not the polite, well-mannered Professors we knew earlier. Students who might earlier have tried to be rude and casual with them, shrank back.

Dr. Sawhney's lectures took on a different hue. He smirked at the students in complete contempt. He still covered the syllabus as required but he compressed an entire hour's lecture in ten minutes, and, what was more, was so amazingly lucid that no questions could possibly be asked.

But the remaining fifty minutes was where the "problem" was.

He introduced an entirely new area of Mathematics to his raw and immature students. He wrote bizarre equations on the blackboard and asked his students to read them out and say a Sanskrit phrase before and after. It was like a language class for primary students. When they did these things, there would be fantastic after-effects.

In one case, the light in the classroom dimmed for several seconds. In another case, an extremely obnoxious smell swept the classroom, followed immediately by the smell of roses. In a frightening incident, Dr. Sawhney's neck was observed to rotate six times. His eyes radiated a blue light. An ostrich walked through the window, walked up the wall and disappeared.

The power of Professor Sawhney's personality was suddenly so extraordinary that his students did not scream or complain or object in any way. No one could do anything.

Professor Sawhney unexpectedly dropped by one evening. I presume he found me friendly and non-interfering. My wife and I had looked after him for several weeks some years ago when he was down with typhoid and he had never forgotten that. I was the communication channel he needed every now and then.

At that moment, I was tinkering with my old camera and had just loaded a new roll of film, a rare luxury for me.

After my wife served him some tea, and the customary small talk was made, she excused herself and left the two of us alone. He came straight to the point.

"Professor," he said, his voice dropping, "I have uncovered equations which are completely beyond the understanding of any of you. Logic falls apart. Night becomes day and day becomes night. Music and silence become indistinguishable. The dead come alive and those alive can taste death and return. Whatever rationality you expect to see from a Mathematician can be safely discarded."

"What do you mean, Professor Sawhney?" I asked, quite petrified.

"Prof. Shashtri and I have discovered the connection between Mathematics and the spiritual world. For the past fifteen years we had been following hints that Dr. Shastri had found in various Sanskrit shlokas. We came close to solving the riddles several times and ultimately found that the answer was likely to be in a cave near Shivgaon. I will not bore with you with how we came to that conclusion. We know everything – and I mean everything."

"How do you mean?"

"I know when you will die, how many great-grandchildren you will have and their names. I know that your wife was unfaithful to you twenty years ago. I know when the next wars will be fought and between who. I know the purpose of the existence of the colony of bees in that tree outside. And all this I know because we have mastered the equations of the Universe."

I could not respond to these preposterous comments, which I somehow found perfectly plausible too, having observed Prof. Sawhney's strange behavior lately.

"What did you find in Shivgaon?" I finally asked, my voice trembling just a little.

"You are not bright enough to understand," he said brusquely, "but in simple terms, we found a cave in which lies the source of all Mathematical knowledge this world claims to possess. When Dr. Shastri and I entered that cave and recited the shlokas he had uncovered and recreated, the astral entities in the cave pulsated in a way that I cannot describe and gave us every bit of Mathematics it had. I do not expect you to believe me. And I do not care either way. But it truly happened. Everything then neatly fell into place – numbers, equations, and techniques for calculations. Entire areas of Mathematics fell apart as being contrived and absolutely worthless. I learnt completely new areas that cause physical phenomenon to happen when corresponding equations are written."

Without waiting for my response, he whipped out a sheet of paper and wrote two equations, one horizontally – *and one vertically in the air above the sheet.* And then he whispered something in Sanskrit.

For two complete minutes, Dr. Sawhney was transformed into the most beautiful woman I had ever seen. There is no point in even trying to describe her. Incredibly lovely eyes, high cheekbones, a femininity that was beyond human capacity – I do not know how I had the presence of mind to whip out my camera and take a photograph.

Dr. Sawhney returned from his transformation. He did not object to the unauthorized photography.

"Now what?" I asked, strangely in control.

"Oh nothing," he said simply. "Dr. Shastri and I are leaving. It's senseless to continue. Now we can do all the things we have wanted to do at a moment's notice. Equations written in multiple dimensions are what I need to master. I am on the verge of fantastic discoveries that idiots like you cannot understand."

He scribbled another equation and muttered something. Prof. Shastri appeared on the sofa to my right. Incongruously, he had a suitcase with him.

"We are leaving for Shivgaon right away. We will reach in exactly one second after I write the right equation. I guess you need to tell the College authorities that we have resigned!"

Prof. Sawhney roared with laughter at his own joke and Prof. Shastri simpered noiselessly too – the first time I had ever seen him do that.

"Thank you and Goodbye," said Prof. Sawhney.

He scribbled another equation and muttered something in Sanskrit again. They both disappeared instantaneously and the smell of jasmine spread through the room.

5

Identity

Two hundred years after the system was put into place, there was some discontent. A67289B sent in a note to the Parliamentary Committee on Identification and Tracking asking that the whole structure be dismantled. He was, of course, hunted down and killed right away. That was the law.

But word did get around. The Government had never realized there was simmering support for such unorthodox and clearly anarchic thoughts. N88991G sent in a deferential note, with clear overtones of sarcasm, extending full support to the existing 'brilliant yet primitive' mechanisms. The Government lawyers looked at it carefully but felt they couldn't do much about it. J59277X wrote to say, that while he had no sympathy for A67289B, it would be a mistake for the Government to apply laws blindly. "There is need," he said, "for us to examine on a regular basis, the question of whether society is changing and whether its needs are changing in tandem." J59277X was imprisoned for a few months.

When he emerged, he was a hero.

But the cat was out of the bag. You couldn't stop people from talking and discussing matters in undertones.

"I want some anonymity and privacy," whispered K62452H. "I don't want to be tracked and hounded every single second."

L75905K snarled angrily, "I have a split personality. I am more than a single number."

Then he slapped B88784Q without cause and kissed his dog a second later, thus making a point of some kind.

Someone was found to have blackened the statue of A21100K, the Father of the Identification System.

The Father's statue had been unveiled with great fanfare more than one hundred and fifty years ago, in honour of the method he had devised, which had made the world singularly more efficient. The bronze statue had looked very imposing in the park right opposite the Parliament. A21100K was shown as a man with a determined chin and bushy eyebrows, wearing a long overcoat. Below him were engraved the words he had made so famous 'One Man, One Number'. He still had a following and a yearly routine was followed where politicians would come in and lay wreaths at the base of his statue.

The blackening incident sent shock waves through society. The Conservatives demanded instant death for those responsible for the desecration. The Liberals, some of whom were suspected of having secret sympathy for the emerging school of thought, claimed that had A21100K been alive today, he would have welcomed debate on the issue.

In a speech noted for its rhetoric and high drama, U00921J, the spokesperson of the Liberals, said dramatically, "I am proud of the system that this Great Nation developed and implemented! My own children U76765A and K99940F are living examples and they too will proudly carry forward the tradition to their children and grandchildren. But if we are truly a free people, as we say we are, we ought to allow people to dissent as long as National Security is not harmed!"

But in an emotional speech, H11430L lashed out at the new thinking. She screamed, shaking her index finger at the Liberals, "What we have today is the budding of anarchy! A21100K had warned about this" – here she broke down – "We owe it to the genius who gave us such a brilliant structure to carry on his legacy!" She ended her speech with the national slogan, 'One Man, One Number' in a choked and emotional voice, saluted the Chair, N46327R, and collapsed in her seat. Her colleagues came swarming to her seat and patted her back and shook her hand. Some shook their fists at the Liberals, who booed.

On TV, the talk shows were humming. One show, hosted by the ever-popular icon, G65656G (often called 'GG' by disrespectful youngsters, who knew they were being cheeky and touching the limits of the law) traced the development of the structure in a special show called 'Origins of the Identification System'. He showed clips from the past where A21100K faced humiliation and censure when he proposed his method. Viewers had tears in their eyes as the barbarism of the period revealed itself in its full ugliness!

In those days, people had names, not identifications. For example, 'Ravi', 'Abdul', 'John', and so on. But it was possible for more than one baby to be named 'Ravi'! In fact, there were thousands of them! In this modern age, it is difficult to believe that such chaos existed. But it did! People had different telephone numbers! Multiple email ids! (Video-ids hadn't been invented yet, and neither had under-the-skin identification chips! God! How did they live?) They could open bank accounts wherever they wanted with different numbers!

Fraud and confusion was common, obviously. Enormous administrative systems had to be created to cope with such thoroughly inefficient social structures. Multiple banks existed; phone numbers changed without reason, people were even allowed to change their names!

One feels a sense of shame in recounting our history, but it is a sign of intellectual maturity to fully confront the ghosts of our past and acknowledge how asinine our ancestors were.

Even the Father, A21100K, had a name. His parents had named him 'Ajay'. In fact, his name was a complex 'Ajay Reddy'. The theory at the time claimed that the 'Reddy' was part of a weak identification system of some kind, but modern sociologists dismiss that as nonsense. All in all, it was another example of perverse self-gratification and a desire to assert uniqueness.

How the man suffered! By the time he was ten years old, he had realized that the system (if you could call it that!) needed to be changed. And so, against all odds, he developed the first version slowly and carefully. In fact, to this day, our current system has a core that is unchanged, which traces back to the original proposals.

He was brave enough to walk up to the Government office when he turned eighteen and ask that his name be changed from 'Ajay Reddy' to '001'. They looked at him as if he was crazy. When he insisted, they called the Police and threw him into jail for being a nuisance. Unwittingly, the case caused a sensation and he received a lot of media coverage. He explained his theory that it would be more efficient if his name were a number, rather than a phonetic mutilation of some kind. Initially, he was treated as an oddity and people scoffed at him. But soon, the theory was widely discussed. After '001' (as he insisted on calling himself in the early days) was released, he wrote papers (preserved today in the National Identification Archives) explaining his theory in depth. A curious millionaire gave him a gift of a million dollars and he had a chip developed, which he said would be implanted in the nostril at birth. The chip would contain all kinds of identification information, such as Blood Type, Parents' numbers, a number by which the baby would thereafter be known as, and so on. The chip caused a sensation. It is hard to believe that there was a violent backlash. In fact, the Father was even physically attacked in those early days! Thankfully, as destiny would have it, he emerged unscathed and lived on to give us what we have today.

The theory extended and expanded. The Government at that time was enlightened enough to allow a trial. Newborn children were given a number, email ids with those numbers were created, telephone numbers with exactly the same number were created and allotted to the baby and a bank account with that number was created automatically.

It was a sensation! What seemed like a fad at the time became a serious movement and more and more people started opting for and demanding numerical names. It took but one generation for ego-satisfying and perverse phonetic names to be discarded completely. People saw the merit of the system and embraced it wholeheartedly. Who could reject a brilliant method that, with one stroke, removed social stratification or origin identification that phonetic names communicated, while bringing every possible government and personal conveniences under one umbrella. "One Man, One Number" – it made total sense!

If you needed to contact someone (say J76450Q) by email, why, all you had to do send it to J76450Q using the mailing program! If you wanted to send money, all you did was transfer it to the Central Account number called J76450Q. If you wanted to speak on the telephone or videophone, all you did was dial J76450Q on your communication handset and you could talk to him or her. Trivial today, but when you think about how novel it must have seemed then, you can understand how and why it was accepted so enthusiastically.

The Father remained humble and retiring till his last days, and steadfastly refused to allow the Government of the day to honour him. When the national system was inaugurated, he applied for and received his identification number like any other ordinary citizen. He received his name A21100K from the Central Office and had the identification chip inserted in his nostril as per the procedure. When he died, the nation was plunged in mourning for a month. A year later, the statue was unveiled. The day was declared a holiday. The masses wept. Scenes of extraordinary emotion were witnessed and are preserved today in the National Archives.

✦

And now! Now! There are some who want to reverse this extraordinarily effective set of mechanism! They claim, the cowards, that this efficient structuring violates the fundamental premise of uniqueness and self-identity. What fundamental premise? And have we all not learnt that self-identity is a purely selfish notion? Imagine salivating over your own NAME! How disgusting!

They also say that they want their chip removed. Pray why? It doesn't harm you. You would want to do this only if you had a devious or destructive intent. It is there for your own safety and well-being!

They say the current identification system violates their privacy and right to anonymity. Whoever said that we had such a right? Of what use is such a silly right? And why are they after privacy? One can only conclude, regretfully, that they want to do something illegal!

We hope that the Government will not succumb to the perverted notions of idle anarchists who are always seeking to introduce disorder and disrespect for our heritage.

One Man, One Number!

6

We are Watching You

I was looking at some books on the rack at my favourite bookstore.

The man next to me on my left spoke in a low whisper.

"We've been watching you for a long time now."

I turned, puzzled.

"What?" I said.

He looked to his left and walked away.

Thinking I had misheard, I continued browsing, a bit disturbed.

From behind me, a woman spoke in a soft hiss.

"Yes, we are watching you. We have been watching you since you were a child."

I whirled around. She had already turned away and moved out. All I could see was a slim woman with greying hair in a brown dress. Then she was gone.

I chose a book and went to pay for it.

As I walked towards the cash counter, those at the counter fell silent. First they looked at me and then at each other. Those in front melted away to give me room.

Everyone stared at me intensely. I thought there was a hint of menace in all those eyes.

I placed the book on the counter without a word and took out my wallet to pay.

The cashier shook his head.

"No," he said.

"No?" I asked.

"No. You can't buy this book."

"What? Why not?"

He shrugged.

"That's what we've been told."

"By whom?"

"Them."

"Who are they?"

"You don't need to know."

"That's nonsense. This is just a Cookery book! How can you refuse to sell to me?"

"Oh no! I'm not refusing to sell to you. In fact, I am supposed to sell you this". He bent below the counter and brought out another book.

"That's exactly the same book that I have here!"

"Maybe. But you can have only this copy and not that one."

"What nonsense!" I sputtered

"Sorry. We do as we are told."

"Yes," said someone behind me. "Buy the book"

"Buy the book," said yet somebody else.

"You must buy the book!" said someone, a little angrily, a little restless.

"How much?" I asked, wishing to get out of the place.

The salesman pulled out a huge calculator and spent several minutes furiously adding and subtracting numbers.

I was about to ask him to look at the price on the book, but I held my tongue.

"It's Fifty Rupees," said the salesman.

"But this copy says it's forty!" I exclaimed.

"You are not supposed to buy that copy!" screamed someone from the back.

I opened my wallet to pay.

The salesman shook his head.

"You can buy the book but you can't pay for it."

My head spun. I said nothing.

"Start the collection," shouted the salesman, addressing a person behind me.

Someone started walking around asking for money.

"One rupee each, please. The time has come."

Without any questions, everyone reached for their money and took out a rupee each.

"Thirty Nine, Forty, Forty One…"

"Here you are," he said to the salesman and handed over fifty rupees.

"Here you are," said the salesman, handing the book over to me.

"Here you are," I said testily, proffering the money to the man who had collected it.

Everyone gasped!

A woman screamed and fainted. No one paid any attention to her.

"It's your book. I am not allowed to take it or read it. Only you can," he said, looking deep into my eyes.

"He needs watching," said someone from the far corner.

"Who is watching me and why?" I screamed.

"He doesn't know," said someone.

"He doesn't know," said another, somehow dejected.

"He doesn't know!" gasped one more, mortified.

"He doesn't know? That's impossible!!!" screamed yet another, appalled by this realization.

"Take your book please," said the salesman firmly, and hustled me outside. "They don't like scenes."

"Who?"

"The persons watching you."

"Who are they?"

He looked at me pityingly.

"Read the book," he said and shut the door.

Inside, all was now quiet and people were busy looking at the books on the shelves.

I opened the book.

All the pages were blank. Except one.

"Look behind you," it proclaimed, in big print.

I looked behind. There was no one.

I looked back at the book. The print had changed.

"Sorry. I meant to your left."

I looked.

A young boy, not more than ten years old, was watching me intently.

"You're being watched," he said.

"By whom?" I asked.

"Oh, by several people," he said, vaguely.

"I've been watching you since I was three," he said, looking important.

"In fact," he said, "many people have been watching you for many years. Probably since you were eight."

"But why???" I asked, horrified.

"You are the reason for their existence. They were born to watch you."

"What nonsense!" I said, scornfully.

"He's right," said a muffled chorus behind me.

I turned around. Everyone in the bookstore had his or her face pressed to the windowpane. They had been watching and listening.

I ran! In my haste and alarm, I dropped the book.

Screams followed me.

"The book! The book!"

"He's left the book behind!"

"Give it back to him! Hurry!"

Everyone streamed out of the store; many were weeping! The boy grabbed the book and ran after me, with everyone else in hot pursuit.

I ran past the other stores in the market! I turned a corner and rushed into a restaurant and into its kitchen at the back. The cook was busy cutting vegetables with great care. He didn't turn.

"I guess they found you," he said quietly, with a sigh.

"Have you been watching me too?" I asked.

"I was. But others wanted to watch you too and I had to give in. Now I'm watching someone else."

"But why???" I asked

"We have to bid to be given permission to watch someone. Others had higher bids and so they bought me out."

"Like an auction?"

"Like an auction."

"But why would anyone want to watch me?"

"There are reasons."

"Tell me!" I begged.

By then the crowd had guessed where I was and I could hear the boy shouting.

"He's in the kitchen! He's in the kitchen!"

I rushed out of the back door.

I ran down the road with the mob in hot pursuit. I turned into a Police Station.

"Help me!" I said to the constable outside, gasping and heaving.

"It's him!" shouted the constable to someone inside.

"Him? It's really him? I must see him!" came many shouts from within.

"What's going on?" I asked, frightened.

"Have you read the book yet?" asked the constable.

"But it's blank!"

"It was. Look inside now!"

The boy had caught up with me and handed over the book. I looked.

I opened a page. Flames shot up. I shut it hastily. I opened another. A great cool breeze wafted up. I opened a third. The smell of mint chutney overwhelmed my senses.

I sat down on a bench. The crowd milled around me.
"Let me look!" shouted one
"It's my turn now!" shouted another.
(ABRUPT MYSTIFYING END OF STORY)

7

Memories of the Living

So much time has passed. Often, I catch myself puzzled by this existence. I move forward and backward and even sideways in time except beyond a point in my past. The point when I entered the world of the dead.

This world, where I am and where I shall always be, is difficult to get used to. When I was alive, I was very apprehensive of what I might find after the exact moment of death. I now find it almost laughable that my mind was filled with escalating, completely uncontrollable fears. Panic, ever rising, almost interminable, all within one frozen second...I look back at that grossly exaggerated moment and laugh. Of course, I am forgiving enough to know that I had been conditioned by a lifetime of experiences, all of which revolved around the apparently final menacing state of death. A body that once moved, twitched, heaved, jerked, twisted and rested for regular intervals, was to become entirely inert, incapable of interaction and response. This change resulted in deep grief to other, similar bodies, which vehemently demanded a return of life and continued experiences with the body in question.

There is almost a film or a one-way glass that allows us, now, to watch those still alive. I do not mean to sound patronizing, but the confusion and chaos of the living that we watch through that bluish film is almost amusing. I feel ashamed and contrite, almost immediately, that I might suppose myself to know something *extra*. I am aware that those beyond the film will one day travel across to us, leaving a physical shell at the threshold, as if on the foot-rug. And then they will know exactly what I do now.

What is equally amusing, is that the very nature of the relationships that we believed would endure past the period of life into the apparent endlessness of the state of the death also evaporates when the transition takes place.

When I was alive, I had a son to whom I was deeply attached. Likewise, he adored me. When I died, I saw his grief was intense and almost embarrassing – to me. On and off, I would see him, rather neutrally, and would see that his memory of me was still sharp enough to bring tears to his eyes, especially when he was alone.

In turn, he too died and joined us. Perhaps he looked forward to being reunited with me, his dear loving father. But yet, when he saw me again, neither of us felt anything special. We were just two entities in a different world that found the very concept of relationships – tender or enduring – quite pointless and ultimately irrelevant. Once, in the living world, I was swept by emotions of love and protectiveness whenever I saw my son, from his infancy to young adulthood. Now I was quite incapable of emotions, which were just not part of us. Nostalgia was bogus.

Here and there are light and darkness in equal measure; it has no significance because we cannot 'see', per se. I dangle in a space of infinite depth below me. How odd it is, that my very individuality persists and others have not subsumed me. Indeed, we do not need to persist or even be absorbed. Time and other norms do not apply. There is no one to please, no one to answer to. There are no expectations. Time and its shadow do not touch us.

Once in a while, a tremor touches all of us. We do not know where it comes from and its purpose. Nothing actually changes. We turn, with unseeing eyes, to where we believe the source is. There is no hint of a threat, because, in any case, we do not hold on to any love for ourselves. We are indifferent to ourselves. How can you threaten the dead?

Sometimes, sound slips in from across the film; I do not know how and why. Even though I cannot hear it, I become aware of it. Pleasure, if any, drives me to attach myself to the sound and ride with it. In relation to the sound, I am static and ought not to feel any different. But I do, and once again, there is no logic.

And in this world, we cannot differentiate. No man, no woman, no humans, no animals. An ant that lived for only eight hours lives easily and comfortably with me. As with everyone else, there is really no need to communicate, no need to share experiences. For there is no purpose.

But yet, although I am blanketed by 'non-emotion', I sometimes do remember my life beyond the film. I observe this memory and wonder at it. If it were irrelevant, why would it exist and why would I be drawn to it?

It might be the memory of an event or a person. Yes, I see this one, with an effort, and a whiff of excitement overcomes me for the briefest of moments. I raise a violin. The muscles of my arms and fingers contract and expand very gently, feeling the pleasure of anticipation. Four strings diverge symmetrically from pegs at a distance. The smell of varnish and rosin touches me strangely. The lovely curves of the violin – I observe them and am not unmoved.

The strings rest on the bridge. The bridge itself exists because of the tension of the strings. Were the strings to slacken, the bridge too would collapse.

If not for the living, would we, the dead, exist?

And now the bow gently sits on the strings and moves. The hair on the bow rubs ever so gently on the metal. At the far end, a finger stirs, moves and comes down at some point on one of the strings. A vibration is born, traveling down the bridge and through the cavity of the violin, amplifying, and then spreading out from the S-holes. Separately, the bow continues moving, inching its way into a direction away from the violin. Other fingers prepare themselves for the task of helping the birth of music. My eyes are glazed and see neither the bow, nor the bridge nor the fingers that move to a separate discipline. The eyes see something else, reminded by sound.

There is no one nearby except a shadow at the far end of the room. It is the shadow of me, separated from the body, taking a life of its own, watching me. For that shadow, I play. The violin glistens, but for whom? The shadow merely listens, and I merely produce music. Though my eyes are closest to the source, it is my ears that benefit.

Such is one memory that still satisfies me, though I am dead. There is no reason.

Indeed, there are many more experiences and thoughts that could be candidates for recollection. But I am indifferent.

How did that last moment come about? Ah, with an effort, I now recall.

Engrossed as I was in my work, reading something, I did not know that a small vein in my right foot had quivered gently for a fraction of a second. That was the signal that the rest of the body had been waiting for, for an entire lifetime. Blood slowed at one place and gushed at another, entirely at random. Nerves folded on themselves. My eyelashes curled and the roots of my hair shrank. My heart sent a sharp stab of pain, absolutely without reason, confusing me. Fear entered, and in that instant, displaced my essence. My body simply gave up control and I collapsed. I found myself halfway through this blue film. I had already discarded my last thoughts of panic and found the whole experience that I had just been through – by this I mean my lifetime – inexplicable, useless and unsatisfying. I entered and looked back through the film, with absolute indifference and almost boredom. It was swift and sure and the transformation was complete almost when it started. I wondered idly at the peculiar physical structure that I had occupied for that period involving the incomprehensible notion called time.

We, the dead. We, the entities that endure. What is our purpose? Perhaps even that is a useless question. Our numbers increase imperceptibly, though there is no crowding since we do not need space. No shape, no balance, no motive, no desire.

Every now and then, as we exist in the most complete of silences, I remember the living. Not always my own memories of my lifetime. How far away, how long ago. I still exist. In front there is nothing. This is not depressing. And yet, it is these select, very brief memories of the time when I was alive that give me a vague sensation akin to pleasure. Yes, indeed, in that sense I am still not dead and may never be.

8

God in a Restaurant

"Only the weak and treacherous believe in God," he declared vehemently.

His friends responded, alternately assenting and shaking their heads. Endless arguments were to begin, never closing, branching out like growing tendrils into areas that none knew of, beyond a few superficialities, which they believed were, in fact, the total. The setting was a small seedy restaurant with cracked plates, dirty faded walls and excellent service.

"Yes," said one, "God is merely a figment of imagination, created by man himself as the end-all and be-all answer to all those perplexing questions that he cannot logically find answers for."

He sat back, overwhelmed by the brilliance of his remarks, hoping that the waiter who had passed by had heard him and relayed the remarks – in awe – to the cook and the others in the kitchen.

"Fool," said another, a believer for the moment, breaking rudely into the momentary stupor that the previous speaker had lulled himself into. "God is around. Be humble. Do you doubt the air you breathe because you cannot see it? Because water has no taste, do you crave it less?" Here he broke into a Sanskrit *shloka*, which suddenly bubbled up into his consciousness from childhood memories, whose meaning he barely understood and was probably completely irrelevant to the discussion. The waiter had just passed by and he hoped that he would report to the cook that he had just served an astonishing intellectual, a man of God, who could smoke and philosophize profoundly at the same time.

Yet another, bearded, who believed that deep silences were the most profound, cleared his throat. He merely said "Hmm...," and he then looked at the window and his eyes seemed to glaze as he apparently thought deep thoughts. Then he shook his head, muttering No, No, as his private intellectual joust resolved itself. From the corner of his eye, he saw the waiter serve the next table within visual and hearing distance. He hoped that the waiter had picked up grave and subtle vibrations from him. Perhaps he would now report to the kitchen that there was a luminous persona at Table Six, whom he had been privileged to witness dissect a question of deep import, which was beyond him, a humble waiter, to actually frame.

The original speaker spoke, not wanting his seminal contribution to be lost on his colleagues – and ultimately on the waiter and all the rest beyond.

"See. Look at that poor woman sitting on the footpath across this restaurant. Of what use is God to her now? Her back is bent, with age and toil; there is no one who finds any value in her. In her eyes is indifference, no longer even measuring the movement of time. She has nothing to cover her ugly feet with cracked soles. She holds a staff merely to support herself. Why would she believe in God?"

He sat back, scarcely believing he had said such lovely words. He noted, with regret, that the waiter was not around to listen; he had disappeared into the bowels of the kitchen to convey an order – or perhaps to educate an awed audience about his brushes with intellectuals, masters of speech and thought.

The Bearded One once again cleared his throat, and after a pregnant six seconds of silence, said, "The staff itself may be considered God, could you not say? It supports her silently and without comment and does not intrude in any manner that she might not want."

The waiter had returned with a new pack of cigarettes he had ordered and had undoubtedly heard him. What might the workers in the kitchen think, to hear such profound concepts? Would they mature in a second, throwing away the web of their humdrum lives and always look back at this moment as the defining one?

And now The Believer said, "Indeed, as Kabir and Surdas have said, God is there in the most unlikely things, always supporting, never abandoning. For the moment, the old woman needs her staff. And in that staff is God. She does not know, because she is simple and merely lives life because she has no option."

He hoped that the waiter, who had returned with an order for another table in the vicinity, had heard his words.

There was no doubt that he would report to the kitchen that there was a Man of Letters at Table Six who knew the ancient scriptures and who was able to find the answers to complex knotty problems that he himself, a mere waiter, could not even fathom.

"Of what use is such a God?" asked the first speaker rhetorically, in a brilliant sally. He was mindful that the waiter must always remember that he had originated the conversation. That he controlled the table and all the thoughts that might surface. "To create and connive in such suffering and then to claim that he will always be there for her? This implies that God has a huge ego. But that makes no sense. Therefore, there is no God."

The waiter was seen to return to the kitchen through the swinging doors, his white hat melting away, but flickering as the doors oscillated, shutting him away one moment and revealing a glimpse the next. Without a doubt, his words had been heard, thought the speaker. Perhaps the waiter was now in deep silence, pondering over the majestic display of logic, finding himself confronted by uncomfortable questions. I hope he does not mess up the order he had just taken because he is lost in thought, thought the speaker, chuckling noiselessly to himself.

The Bearded One cleared his throat. The rest waited, most impatiently, because he was going to upstage their own deep verbalizations with banal words that they found annoying and needlessly provocative. They noted, privately and resentfully, that the waiter had returned and so the timing was perfect.

"You are right. And you are wrong. In the old woman sitting there in the dirt and grime of this anonymous filthy road, perhaps we see God in a way that none of us is prepared well enough to cope with. We have been so deeply conditioned about God, that, try as we might, we cannot shake away the image of him as a benevolent puppeteer alternately punishing and rewarding, illogically. What events must she have witnessed in her life? Quite similar to so many others, and yet uniquely different. We dare not pretend that we might have answers to the unresolved questions of her life."

He stole a furtive glance at the waiter who was now at their table. He hoped that the waiter would recognize and report the existence of a man of deep compassion and understanding, of great tolerance.

The waiter had presented a bill to the small group. "Thirty Six Rupees, Sirs," he said.

He waited as the friends contributed their fair share and totaled it up.

"That's Thirty Five only, Sirs."

"Oh?" said one, looking away.

"Hmm," said another absorbed in thought.

"I know!" exclaimed the first speaker, thrilled by the joke he was about to crack. "Ask that old woman sitting outside to give the rest!"

"Yes!" said the bearded one, warming to the idea. "She has provoked so many thoughts in us. She cannot do that for free!" He laughed a deep hollow laugh that seemed to roll gently around the room pushing its way through the revolving door that led to the kitchen perhaps to be heard by the cook and his workers.

The waiter was silent for a few seconds. Then he spoke.

"I cannot do that, Sirs."

"She is my mother. She is waiting for me. She has no money."

9

The Destruction of His Ego

As the evening prayers at the monastery came to a close, the monks slowly opened their eyes to return to the present. The serene silence within spoke of great peace. The incense wafted across the large prayer hall and high up to the ceilings, calming the senses of the monks and the ordinary men and women who had come to meditate and find solace. Slowly, everyone dispersed, without the slightest sound.

An old man, about sixty-five, wearing nondescript clothes, stood up and walked across to where the Head Monk sat. He prostrated and sat with his thighs on his calves, resting on his knees and toes. He placed his hands on his knees, his eyes respectfully on the ground.

After five minutes, the Head Monk opened his eyes and spoke softly.

"Speak, what can we do for you?"

"I wish to suppress and destroy my ego completely," the man replied.

"I see," said the Head Monk.

After another five minutes, the man spoke.

"I have lived a full life. I have fame, power, and money. I have children and grandchildren. I have a loving devoted wife. I now wish to prepare for death."

"Have you known grief?"

"Perhaps much less than most people."

"Without experiencing grief, it is not possible to destroy your ego. Experience it, and then return."

The man withdrew respectfully.

He returned after several months.

"Well?" he was asked.

"Yes, I have experienced grief. My grandchildren died. And so did my wife."

"Anything else?"

"Yes, I lost my entire fortune."

"Very good."

"I seek knowledge and strength to cope with my losses."

After a long silence, the Head Monk said, "Your ego still exists. You are still worried about your own well-being. Work for the happiness of others without expecting to be observed and praised, without expecting recognition. Work in darkness where you will not be seen performing good deeds."

The man withdrew respectfully. He gave away his clothes to the first beggar he met. He handed over his wallet to his driver and asked him to take away the car. He walked for several days to a city far away where he was sure that no one would know him. There he worked in the slums, doing anything he possibly could to help anyone who needed it. He cleaned toilets, he slept on pavements, and he ate only if he was offered anything by anyone. He removed unclaimed dead bodies to the crematorium and performed their last rites. He hugged dying dogs and comforted them till they died. He fed rats. He washed his body only when it rained. Disgust went away when he lived in filth. With disgust went away the fear of the unknown. Shame left him too. His own sorrow crept away from him as he attended to the miseries of others.

After several months he returned to the Monastery.

"Can I now conquer my ego?" he asked the Head Monk.

"The very fact you asked that question tells me you still have an ego and wish for something for yourself. Think about it and come back after six months," said the

Head Monk.

The old man respectfully withdrew again and walked away slowly to a completely different town.

There, he continued doing what he had been doing earlier. He cut down on his needs even further. He ate next to nothing and even that, only at night, when no one was watching and could have no chance to feed him out of pity. He ate only if his eating would help someone else. Whatever he found or was given he gave away immediately and left before he could be thanked, because that would have caressed his ego. When asked his name, he did not answer but turned and walked away. He stopped talking because words are an expression of the self – either a longing or a question needing an answer or an opinion signifying individuality or a response indicating existence. He covered his eyes, because to see would be to invite thought and comparison. He blocked his ears to prevent himself from responding or to be swayed by laughter or cries of misery. He worshipped dogs and stones and prayed that the egos of others be erased. He no longer knew who he was.

At the end of six months, the monks waited for the old man to come to them for advice. No one came. After a few days, the monks conferred and arrived at a decision. They divined the location of the old man. Then they shut down the monastery and walked in a slow silent procession to the city where he lived. They found him living in a filthy ditch surrounded by rats in the middle of a stinking, noisy, busy street.

He did not acknowledge the respectful greetings from the Head Monk. All the monks sat down in the muck on the road and the Head Monk then prostrated himself at the feet of the old man. "Please teach us how to eliminate our egos."

In answer, the old man got up and walked away. To teach was to imply greater knowledge. Such awareness would revive his ego. He was no longer interested.

10

Within My Depths

I would not advise you to consider any kind of deep exploration into your recesses unless you know what you are doing.

Have you wondered what the term 'soul-searching' actually means? Perhaps you thought it meant being honest with yourself? I'm not very sure if that is true. It may simply mean a very deep and intense survey of what lies within – but getting there is not for everyone. It is not a joke or an exciting exercise to talk about later or an immature dalliance with spiritual concepts.

I found this out the hard way.

I had foolishly advertised to the world my interest and shallow knowledge of 'occult' matters. I was an imbecile. It was a silly way to draw attention to myself and push aside my insecurities. There were many who were taken in by my masterful way of conducting Meditation classes. I used big words and spoke softly. I talked of peace and love. I hinted that I was a great Guru, reluctantly dragged into this world because God had a plan for me and wanted me to serve others. It wasn't too bad. I was an honest man, and actually did believe in simple living. I locked myself in my bedroom for hours and claimed to be meditating and reciting the name of God.

My father was scornful. He shouted at my mother for tolerating my nonsense and often asked me to continue my studies and get married. "This fool does not know what he is doing!" he proclaimed. "He does not know a thing about these matters and is totally unqualified to talk about the occult, Devils and Gods!"

I mouthed a sermon of peace and the virtues of doing away with anger, and stepped back into my bedroom where I lit some incense.

My Father finally disappeared for a few days saying he had had enough and he would solve the problem very soon. He came back with G__, a persona from his ancestral village.

G__ was a small man, sitting cross-legged on our sofa, looking quite out of place. He seemed unwashed, with a three-day stubble. He seemed to be constantly licking his lips.

"Touch his feet, he is a great enlightened soul," my Father commanded.

Ho hum. One more of my Father's specimens, I thought. But anyway, I did as he bid.

G__ touched me on my head.

Something travelled from my scalp to my toes.

I looked up, startled. G__ wasn't smiling. In fact, his face was expressionless. Already, his gaze had wandered off elsewhere.

I retreated from the room in some confusion.

My Father followed, puzzled. "Why did you leave like that?" he asked.

"I felt very strange," I replied. "That man is disturbing". I was surprised to notice my voice had a quaver.

My father looked at me curiously. With a vague half-smile, he returned to the drawing room. I went to the kitchen, feeling slightly confused and breathless, and sat heavily on a chair.

After a while, they seemed to be exchanging pleasantries and promises to meet again soon and I then heard the front door close. G__ had left.

"Is something wrong?" asked my Father rather calmly.

"I feel very sleepy," I replied, barely able to speak. I found I couldn't get up without help. My Father seemed alarmed, but he helped me up and we went to my bedroom. I collapsed in a heap.

"Shall I call a Doctor?" he asked anxiously.

"No, no. I just need a nap," I whispered.

I lay on my back, the hair on my arms and legs slowly rising and falling. The light in the room seemed to dim perceptibly. My Father's face seemed to fade. His voice seemed to be calling from a great distance and was going further and further away. Everything converged to a smaller and smaller point. My breathing became shallow and muted. I seemed to relax and slowly sink into something pleasurable. It was a very conscious feeling of 'sleep'.

G__ stood outside our gate, motionless, his eyes closed.

✦

I have now drifted one layer below the conscious level. About me is a peculiar murmur and weightlessness. A haze of light seems visible just above the clearly distinguishable separating layer between where I was and where I am. I twist and turn very slowly and without effort. I peer down at the darkness of the layers that beckon below, inviting me to dive in. I can hear an urgent shouting. I control the breathing of the body to which I belong, though I have somehow separated from it, while still being trapped within it.

I now slowly move down one more level. I am reminded of a hot-air balloon descending through layers of air. As I now enter this new layer, there is great calm and quiet around. The ink-black surroundings seem very safe. I can see very well indeed and there is a great sense of peace. I did not know that within me, there had been such depths and layers that invited exploration. I am still conscious of my heart beating gently in the distance. I close my eyes and then close them again and again. Each time I do so, it seems that I sink in an inch more into the comfortable zone of blackness. Something profound is going on.

I now feel a sense of imbalance. I seem to be tilting and falling in a controlled and predictable way. I follow the sensation calmly with a mild interest. What will happen next?

Now there is a sea of white light through which I drift. I cannot tell if it emerges from me or is being absorbed. My breath is suspended and I watch myself curiously from many angles. I seem to be stretched in every direction in a soft and pleasant way. An aroma of absolute peace moves in and out of my nostrils with no persuasion. I continue to shrink and converge to a point somewhere.

I have now burst out with no resistance into a small core within me. Is this the last layer? Colours dance about and an understanding pervades this core. This capsule enunciates soft singular syllables of what seems to be Nature in its absolute essence. My eyes close and close again, retreating into this... this something. Some layer has been gently removed and I hear music that I had always known existed, but which I had never heard consciously.

Here many like myself join me. I look about with great joy and extreme clarity. Pleasant others move about, acknowledging my entry with what seems a smile, though it cannot be as there is no form. All seem happy to be here, where there is a final sense of purpose and meaning. How come they are within me? On the other hand, could I have entered them, while still being within myself? I brush aside these idle thoughts and move quietly and without purpose, content with the knowledge of having reached some apex of experience and understanding.

Space has compressed within, time has distilled, and there is a great and extravagant expanse of peace.

All of a sudden, I feel myself being seized very roughly. There is a violent disturbance. There are ripples about me. Sounds have become skewed and distorted. Though there is no physical form, I have been paralysed by a collection of noxious sounds and smells. I am assaulted and I feel the pain very acutely. This happens without any actual movement. A sharp instrument, invisible and totally independent of any guiding force, slowly starts the process of skewering me. The pain is extraordinary, the humiliation intense. All about me, I hear only contemptuous jeers. I am unable to even ask for help, and so I submit to this barbaric subjugation and flaying. And all this is happening within me!?

"Who asked you to come here?" says an angry voice formed of the very same sylph-like syllables I had admired a moment ago.

I am unable to answer.

"This section is off-limits without permission. This part belongs to all of us, but not to you."

I can make no sense of what this means.

"Those who intrude cannot be permitted to live or die. To die is to allow the law to be broken. To live is take back our secrets."

Many beings jab their invisible rapiers into me, one without form, who can still feel unimaginable pain. I am now twisted and turned forcefully and pushed to an invisible corner with very sharp edges. A sudden vacuum leaves me breathless, while angry laughs sweep over me. I try to close my eyes again but fail.

"You cannot do that anymore," says someone distinctly but tersely. "This is it, no more."

"How dare you come here?"

"I...just ...just ...came."

A liquid is poured over me, scalding me in a horrific way.

A sense of terrific speed overcomes me as I am thrown over a vast distance, into the arms of a different set of...*things*. They seem to grope me with rough members of some sort, with no wish to be gentle or careful. I am torn apart piece by piece, and I am fully conscious of the act. My consciousness is split amongst all these parts and somehow still retains a sense of the whole. Then they proceed to put me back together in a random manner and this act now distorts that sense of being 'one'.

"How dare you come here?" demands a new voice alternately shrieking and growling.

"I did not know...." I say it but I do not know how.

"Yes, you know! You knew there was something that was hidden. You thought you would come and discover something, which you had a right to. In fact, you have no right!"

"Did it occur to you that it was hidden for a reason?"

"No."

My answer infuriates them and they lash out, disintegrating me and then subjecting me to unimaginable pain. There is no body, no physical entity and still they ensure that I suffer. I cannot react and I am struck dumb by the sheer beauty of the pain. They sense this response and are further angered.

But suddenly, a peculiar pink blankets us and I feel a sense of relief. Now I feel surrounded by entities of innocence. They touch me and sing soft soundless songs, as though comforting me. They murmur and speak soothingly.

"No, no. You should not have come. This is not the place for you."

"You are not ready. Do not try things that you are not ready or qualified for. "

"You cannot understand this place, as your soul is not ready."

"Oh, how sorry we are that you suffered!"

"But is it not me that I am exploring?" I somehow manage to ask.

"Oh no! Oh no! This is not a dimension to which you have any access! Do not attempt such experiments. We cannot save you again!" they say in a chorus-like sing-song lament.

I am now escorted upwards; the journey is swift but long. The layers seem the same but are different. At different layers, others take over the task of taking me to the next. A feeling of great peace pervades my invisible cells.

✦

G__ now opened his eyes, looked at our house and walked away.

I woke with a start to see my Father sitting by me, looking at me anxiously. His relief on seeing me recover was palpable.

He did not ask any questions. Somehow I suspected he knew. G__ was never mentioned. Was G__ perhaps brought over to teach me a lesson?

I would not advise you to consider any kind of deep exploration into your recesses unless you know what you are doing. Assume nothing. Live a normal boring life and do not let your interest in spiritual matters go beyond a point. There are unknown depths within us that are best kept that way.

11

The Father

Where have the children gone? Where shall I look?

Etched against the darkness in my heart, I see from the corner of my eye a darker image, a silhouette. As I turn to look more closely, it vanishes quickly, unwilling to withstand my gaze and the accompanying beam of surging love.

"I shall not be seen," it says solemnly. "I shall not let you love me. It would hurt me."

"Shall I close my eyes?" I ask.

"It will make no difference," it says.

In the sky, I see an eagle floating mindlessly on the wafts of warm air. But its eyes are ever alert, searching for something alive, something that was loved, to swoop on and eviscerate. A calm silence descends on me and fills my heart.

I see a new image, a little bolder, that lingers to accept my gaze. I cannot see, but she looks at me with large serious eyes. Her hands are clasped together; her chubby fingers locked, perhaps in exasperation, having to deal with the uncomprehending, irritating love of me, her father.

"When will you be back?" I ask.

"Why must I?" she replies. "I am not yours."

And she turns and floats away.

I look at the lines on my palms as they move restlessly like thin worms, adjusting my fate and creating new mysteries for palmists to brood over. The future is now past. And the blazing sun above beats down even more black.

I hold the picture of the children between my thumb and index fingers. It flutters in the breeze, asking for freedom. I let it go. And it does. Moving lazily but surely away. Even though the breeze stops, it moves high and fast. Till it falls on the bough of a dying tree.

But now the tree shakes off its preoccupation with extinction, and green leaves spurt out without warning. But only on that bough where the photograph lies.

My feet ask that they move. I walk towards the source of darkness. Behind me, the branches bend in a goodbye, uselessly, because I cannot see.

12

To Live Again

Dark clouds fill my mind. I am full of foreboding. I know that the end is near but that is not what I am afraid of. As my body slowly but steadily yields to the inevitable pressure of time, as each cell reluctantly gives up that energy which gives it life, my soul stirs and readies for its journey.

My fingers and toes grow cold and the blood in them slows down till it barely moves. My hair itself feels weighed down and seems absolutely exhausted. It begs for the comfort that gravity seems to offer. My earlobes feel heavy and the muscles just beneath my skin lose interest in wanting to be together. My eyeballs, weary with exhaustion, ask, with whatever energy they might still have, if they might disconnect and simply fall into their sockets. My teeth do not wish to be tied to my jaws anymore. My heart itself is too tired to even ask that it be allowed to rest in peace after years and years of loyal service.

I can sense shapes about me. No, not the attendants who foolishly try to keep me alive. There are others. They have no shape, no form. They wait for me with amusement. They have plans for me, for that soul that is twitching inside, trying to break free from the cord attached to my body. Dull low sounds reverberate.

Hisses. Then far away, a thin agonized yodel. Sometimes all together. Something, somewhere is readying itself for me.

I feel myself going through a yawning cylinder. The lights are dazzling at the fringes, but rapidly disappear to a *visible* darkness. Strange colours merge and then dissipate. And even within these throbbing mosaics are those beings that wait. I can see them. I can sense them.

I watch from afar as a strange luminous projection from my body stretches out and probes the area around. The beings shrink away from it but return the moment it moves away, almost giggling. The sounds continue to come and go in disconnected and irregular waves. Yes, I am at the point of death, but I still resist. I do not like what I see and now have second thoughts about whether there really is a heaven, a world of happiness and eternal bliss.

The hair on my body seems to rise and stiffen. On my now gray arms and colourless chest. On my sheet-white cheeks. A slight shudder goes through each limb and shakes away the shapes that wait like invisible vultures waiting for bits and pieces of whatever energy still exists in my drained body. Even now my lungs work, imperceptibly. Near my nostrils, the dark and invisible clouds stay away, not liking the heat. I am not yet ready. And they grow impatient. They have waited years and years for this moment and they do not like my little game, my delaying tactics. They are annoyed but can do nothing.

Can I change my mind? It is almost impossible to summon the energy to think, but I manage to do it. I decline to die.

And as that thought, as that declaration is made across my being, the shapes howl with anger and fury and step away to their usual distance, several feet away, where they will continue to watch for me to wage my final battle.

13

When I Slept

I have watched myself go to sleep. Several times. Hovering about a foot above my body, I have watched the last twitches of my tired body longing for an escape from reality – sleep. I have restlessly shifted from side to side, adjusting the bed sheets around me, sometimes on my back, sometimes on my side, and often on my stomach. I have watched myself clutch the pillow and adjust my head till the feeling was just right.

Then I have welcomed myself into this other reality. I am never surprised to see myself again, unfailingly. It could almost be considered peculiar, to hold my own hand and walk with myself into that space of illogic. But when we dream, we let completely random images, situations and consequences waft in from unexpected directions and are never caught off guard. We are never baffled.

A tenuous umbilical cord of electrons ties me to my physical self. It stretches at length, coiling, twining and wafting in the bluish-purple haze. And when we choose to close any particular 'voyage', the cord draws my own self back into the physical world, leaving me to watch myself separate.

We went together into that tunnel, I and I. On the left was a curved wall heading skyward. The wall felt smooth and cool at one point. At another, the face of a young girl stared at me with blank eyes. I had seen her somewhere – or had I?

On my right was a landscape full of gardens, sand, tall golden trees, birds with three wings, and a huge Mercedes-Benz car changing colour rapidly. We had no comment to make.

We ran into an old acquaintance. It was the sister of a girl I had wanted to marry years ago. She asked me if I had written my Mathematics examination yet. We realized we had not. We tried to run, but each movement was intensely difficult. We finally reached, but the exam was halfway over. We looked at the paper but had no idea what to do. I started singing loudly. It did not appear to disturb the other students who quickly finished answering the questions and left. The lady in charge of the exam came over and gave me a violin to tune. We tried our best. Much later we realized that the violin had no strings, but by then it was too late. The room was on fire and the flames were advancing menacingly towards me. I took off my shirt and the flames died down.

I asked the three Chinese men who were standing behind me if was time to eat. They walked past me without even a look. I was drawn to them. I kept asking them if I could eat. They did not reply. I hit them. It made no difference. I started to cry with frustration.

Now we found ourselves sitting quietly under a tree. As I looked up at the leaves, some of them came together and formed a human face – it was of my neighbour, a woman from many years ago. The leaves fell down slowly into my lap and looked up at me. I tried to kiss them but it just didn't work. I tried and tried but the leaves were always an inch away, though they were in my hands.

The cord suddenly tugged. I separated from myself wordlessly. I watched myself enter my physical body. My body stirred and opened its eyes. I looked up and saw myself drift away.

14

The Messenger of Death

From afar, I have seen him, the Messenger of Death.

Hooded, face hidden, with a stick in his hands, he moves slowly towards me on a slim strip of light. A demented orgy of day and night swirls around him and me. And I stand naked, head held high, waiting for him to come close, lift a bony finger and lightly poke my chest, claiming me.

But I have to wait. Laughing babies swish madly about in the air, cherubic, innocent, full of the new life they have just received. Slowly vibrating sounds that become wet liquids glacially move about with no source and no purpose. They are not pleasant to hear but not unpleasant either. While I watch him, calm and collected, memories of my life gone past surge without warning and without reason. I watch, detached, as one failure dissolves into another. A few moments of pure joy merely give me the energy and stamina to relive the more acute moments of pain.

And now at this time of indifference, when all have slowly moved their fingers away from mine, when my utility has eroded, I do not feel bitter. What do I feel? I am bemused, that I, who now face the final moment of a warped life, stumbling again and again, could have meant something to some people for moments of time. As they stumbled, did I hold them up, for them to say thanks, move on and disappear forever? Within me, my spirit shrank and shrank. Even when I thought it impossible, it shrank some more after the next obstacle, placed by me with my own hands, at some other point of time.

Weary, no longer wanting to endure existence, I sat on my haunches, my eyes closed, trying to block memories and trying to will the closure of my existence. Someone raised me up and gently disappeared without waiting for my wordless thanks.

My ego, my blanket, had been frayed and torn apart. There was nothing to cover me, nothing to hide. I was free, crippled by failures and scarred by betrayal. I was actually happy enough to be calm. I looked behind me and saw successful phantoms move about, glowing with satisfaction. Around them were families, children, friends, all adoring. Around me – there was no one, but I did not grieve. Because there would be no one to grieve for me. I thought that was wonderful, for some reason.

The heat of the Sun beat upon my back, urgent and harsh. I observed the sensations without interest. I looked down at my toes. The nails were slowly melting, painlessly.

When I looked up, he was there, much closer. I looked, with curiosity one moment and with indifference the next. Incongruously, he extended his hand and dropped the photograph of a woman. I had never seen her. She meant nothing to me. I let the photograph slip through my fingers. We watched each other. I, with boredom. He, perhaps, with equal disinterest. Behind him, the inky blackness became thick and viscous, swirling very, very slowly. My limbs felt light, my head clear and calm.

I saw him extending a finger at my chest. The wind whistled shrilly about my ears and I closed my eyes.

15

Planes of Existence

There it was again. A peculiar dream, and, like all such dreams, strangely vivid and incomprehensible. With events and people floating in and out, connecting without reason, dissolving before you could focus on anything. And of course, like all good dreams, finishing before you came to the climax, whatever it was.

I remembered the details even though there was no reason why I had to. For one, the dreams were in colour. The background was a surreal, light blue with a throbbing life of its own. The characters themselves were either bright red – almost crimson – or just a slate gray. I never felt repulsed by the automatic assumption that this signified blood or the pallor of death. Everything didn't need an explanation. It just – was.

There were tears in the eyes of the men, heavy tears, almost viscous, which never dropped to the ground. They never tried to wipe them away. None stood erect; all slouched as though their existence had ground them to the earth. As though life had defeated them and their existence was part of a grand master plan of torture.

The women were always moving. None were beautiful and yet the eyes of the men seemed to gravitate towards them and keep them in focus constantly.

Were they important? Who could say? The women were not feminine. Their eyes were hard, yet with life of a certain ruthless kind in them.

The children were shrinking away from them and yet being dragged along, almost as though trapped by a vicious magnet. In their eyes, in their limbs, their gait – you could see a primal fear. It seemed obvious and not surprising that they would occasionally play a game of snooker before returning to their relentless orbits around their mothers. Dreams, in themselves, are obvious. The analysis, afterwards, rejects them.

The animals were all dead. And they appeared again and again. A dead dog on the road. Another in a jack-knifed posture across a bench in the park. A calf rotting in a ditch with its tail oddly lifted and hanging limp just over the edge. All their eyes were open. They were dead and yet, they were crying. Preposterous.

Whenever I awoke from these recurrent dreams, I noticed that my heartbeat was abnormally fast. I would not be sweating. I would look around wondering if I was still in the dream hoping for the story of that dream to come to its conclusion, whatever it was. And, as you know, one never does reach a climax in a dream, unless it's of a sexual kind.

The morning was unusually heavy and stagnant. Or perhaps it just reflected my own state. The sounds of birds just outside seemed harsh and mocking. The ceiling fan moved slowly, laughing at me with its deliberate clack-clack. A gecko darted across the wall, stopped and stared at nothing. Without warning its tail fell off. I remember thinking that their tails were supposed to fall off only if they are being pursued. So that they could escape. The gecko just stayed put. I saw its tongue flick out lazily and grab an insect that flew by, too close.

I went to the bathroom to brush my teeth, following the set pattern of years of existence. I squeezed some toothpaste on the brush. With half-closed eyes, I looked towards the mirror as I put the brush into my mouth.

It was not my reflection that looked back.

A young boy stared out, his eyes open, as if in shock. I remembered having seen him in my dream, though I could not recall what his role had been. He wore a green collarless shirt, revealing a thin neck with purple veins. He was unremarkable in his looks, with a weak mouth and eyebrows that met in the middle. He had that slate-coloured pallor that I remembered distinctly from my dream. I could only see his bust, of course. I did get a feeling that he wasn't of my time. He was about fifteen years old with a moustache that was struggling to emerge. He then looked down at his left hand and I saw him raise a violin to his chin. With the other hand he raised a bow.

I saw that the violin was very old with curves and tracings from a different time. The dust of years of rosin was sprinkled on the ebony and the wood near the bridge. I saw that the strings were of that same crimson color from my dreams. And

I saw that the bow was made of bone. A very unusual one, with intricate geometrical carvings. Hexagons within squares inside triangles. Lines that were parallel at one end of the bow and converged at the center and then diverged again at the other end. At the end of each line was a satyr, each of whom was looking at me and smiling. I remember these details.

With his right arm raised, he started playing. Music came out from the mirror. Pathos, indescribable emotions, serene lonely notes pulsating for completion while they extinguished the previous ones brutally. The violin itself changed color, moved by this extraordinary display of beauty and ugliness, of hate and love, of venality and tenderness, that it had helped bring to the world. The world as it was.

Then he finished and lowered the violin and the bow.

For a wordless minute, we looked at each other.

Then he shrank slowly to a point, while at the same time, another figure grew slowly from a speck.

And that figure was my own reflection.

And that reflection was smiling.

While I was not.

16

Coming Home

I have known no peace since we met. My heart slows and quivers with pain and longing. My eyes go wet with unwelcome tears. My arms strain against the invisible steel ropes of circumstances that reduce me to helplessness.

After years of meandering through the lazy roads of existence – which pretended to offer me choices – pulled along by time, tripped by relationships and enticed by the flowers of transient pleasures, I had found myself deeply unsatisfied. The sense of being quite alone in my life's journey – I had never been able to reconcile to that. Doubtless, others faced similar dilemmas – but most had ceased to give it thought, and they responded instantly to the relentless knockings of lifetime experiences. Somehow, when something happened that could be called an experience, I simply sat back and dully observed it without even curiosity. I avoided responding to anything. Anything, of any magnitude, I reduced to an inconsequential ripple in the larger scheme of existence. I felt I was a molecule of no weight and declined to participate actively anymore in "life".

I moved with the winds and the tides and did not protest.

I knew I was lonely. Yes, this larger philosophical detachment was a manifestation of extreme depression.

I then met her, quite by accident. I was walking slowly on a sidewalk, with my head down as usual, unimpressed by the sound and sensation of my heart beating on stubbornly. Someone seemed to call out to me to stop, even though there was no sound. I looked around and saw her walking behind me, in much the same way as I had. Clutching a shopping bag to her chest, walking slowly, head down, lost in her own thoughts. Had her thoughts collided with the echoes of my own, left behind in my wake?

I watched her in a daze as she slowly walked towards me. I stepped to one side to let her pass, which she did. But then she stopped and was still, too overwhelmed by whatever thought had elbowed its way so cruelly through her mind. I wondered what she was thinking of and I wondered at the sudden surge of grief that exploded in my throat.

She turned slowly and looked at me. I saw her thin arms and fragile fingers holding on to her bag. I saw her lovely large eyes vandalized by pain and hopelessness.

"I am alone," she said. Even her voice seemed to come from far away, a thing of great beauty, a witness to tragedy and suffering, frightened and haunted.

I reached out and she handed over her bag wordlessly for me to hold. We walked together, silently, slowly.

We sat down on the bench on the sidewalk, not alone anymore. But rather than joy, our sorrow had multiplied. It was the additional sorrow of not having found the other much earlier. I saw she was ill and had little time.

As the evening drew to a close, we got up, not having exchanged a single word. I walked with her to my home, which was now hers as well. She sat on the sofa as though she had known it, its contours, its colours, its touch, for years. I sat at the other end.

Slowly, she seemed to faint, and swayed in my direction. I did not move. Her head gently dropped into my lap, softer than a feather.

Eyes shut, barely breathing, but with a hint of drying tears across her eyelashes, her face colourless, she rested her head on my thigh, as though we knew each other for years.

Her skin was pale and crinkled. I caressed her hand, as it lay limp. She descended further into herself, her vitality reducing to almost nothing, almost merging with the sofa. I saw time replay itself on her face and I saw her as a baby, a girl, and then a woman, ageing rapidly. Ah, I wish I had shared those times with her. She had been made for me but we had never known.

But she had come home. To me. To eternal rest in the arms of an anonymous man made for her. Nothing else mattered; the suffering, the abject loneliness, the constant searching. These moments had more time in them than the years that had passed without the other.

✦ ✦ ✦

17

The Obsession

Time was running out.

The Old Man shuffled to the small cabin behind his house that was his workshop. It was bitterly, numbingly cold outside. Snow had drifted down relentlessly overnight and came up to his knees. And the cold wind almost froze his breath as he exhaled. Icicles formed in almost no time on his eyebrows. He dug his hands deeper into his jacket and plodded on.

He opened the door and walked in, with the fierce wind protesting behind him, dragging him out, wanting to hug him in a fatal embrace. He pushed the door shut behind him and locked it. He turned on the light and looked at his workshop as he rubbed his hands to get the blood circulating again.

In the dim light, he could see the table where he had worked and worked for seventy long years. Wood shavings were piled high in various corners. Their sweet smell – how familiar and welcome it was even after all these years! His tools were stacked neatly in their usual place against the wall just above his table. The Masterpiece was wrapped carefully in an old cotton cloth.

A mouse darted across the floor to the other wall where his works of Art were hung. One on every nail. Lovely violins. Each was his child. They all had personalities and he had always been able to predict how they would end up being as he had started working on the wood.

The Spruce and Maple that went into his violins still came from his old friend's farm in Germany. Every year, without his prompting, two large blocks of wood would arrive. They were large enough to make about six violins over the year. The payment? One Violin a year. That's what his friend demanded and that's what the Old Man sent cheerfully. Year after year after year. Letters were never exchanged. But all the news that was to be said was hidden in the blocks of wood that came one way and the solitary violin that went the other way.

He knew that his friend had been ill for a long time the past year. He had received news of his friend's wife's death. And that one son had been killed in an accident. He knew all this by just caressing the block of wood.

In the violin he made and sent back, the Old Man would hide *his* news. When his friend touched the violin, strung it and played it, he would know exactly what had happened to the Old Man the past year. There was news of his old sheepdog dying in his arms. There was joy that his grandson had had a baby! There were memories of his boyhood days that had suddenly made him nostalgic. And even the fact that the Old

Man remembered playing with the pup his grandmother had given him when he was a boy of five.

And so the two friends had communicated. For sixty-five years now! Yes, a very long time indeed! And so, if you just calculated the numbers, you would see that the Old Man had probably made about four hundred violins. But that would be wrong. This was just the number of violins from his friend's wood. He had made a thousand more violins from other pieces of wood.

He refused to sell them. They were his children. The Old Man made a hard living selling the vegetables he grew during the short spring and summer. Or the wood he would sell by cutting down one or two trees in his large farm. That was enough. A cow, some hens and a few dogs completed the rest of his family. He didn't need to sell the violins. They were his. Do people sell their children?

The Old Man looked at his shimmering violins on the wall. His life went by his eyes. He saw his youth and then his young happy wife, who gave birth to a son and a daughter and then died when she was barely twenty-five. The memories of his children growing up, going to school, finding their mates and making their own lives came bubbling up.

His first grandson! Even now he smiled in delight! The happiest memory of all! How he had loved the little fellow! He would make him laugh by rubbing his beard on his tummy! He would let him pull his moustache! They would play secret games in their hideaway in the woods beyond! And that little fellow – why! He had his own son now! Had it all really happened?

These children on the wall – they were temperamental too! He had to speak to each of them every day! They all had names! They had their moods! They had their friends! He had to place each violin in exactly the right place. If he made a mistake, he would know immediately when he walked into the workshop the next day. He would sense a restlessness and irritation in the air. And it would persist till he corrected his error and consoled the violin.

They needed care. Every other day, he would take a soft cloth and gently remove the fine layer of dust that might have built. Each violin had strings and so he would have to check to see if it was perhaps time to change them. If he did not and the strings rusted, the violins would cry with discomfort. Then he would have to patiently lift them to his chin and run a bow on them and make music and tell them it was all a bad dream. And like small children, they were comforted and slept peacefully.

The Old Man was not a very good violinist. In fact, he had never learned how to play. But he knew enough to extract emotion. He knew exactly which note to play and what each violin wanted him to play. Each presented him with a melody that was its own special signature. When he played that melody, its personality showed itself radiantly.

For some, especially the younger violins, joy and mirth had to be brought out. Mischievous tunes, teasing ones, playful ones, straddling several octaves at the same time. Notes would play hide and seek and shout with laughter when they found each other!

The feminine ones were coquettish. You had to handle them chivalrously and gently. For them to show themselves required coaxing and persuasion. But when they came out – they were like Ballerinas, the notes pirouetting and bending in ecstasy. Sultry notes promising secret pleasures beckoned, and the Old Man was embarrassed to hear them. But each child was different and he had to help them discover themselves and be what they were meant to be.

Some revealed shades of evil when he played them. He would remonstrate and correct them, but when you are something at a basic level you cannot change. The notes they produced were subtle, almost secretive, conniving and plotting. There was always a hint of something extra, which he could never extract.

And then there were the philosophers. Convinced that they held secrets to a hidden world. When the Old Man played them the heaviness of existence weighed upon his shoulders. Tears would roll down his cheeks as each note flowed sublimely with extraordinary purity. Life and death completely suffused the violin and he felt a strange heat coming from it. It seemed to metamorphose and change shapes and all he could do was bow. They knew too much. They were absolute geniuses. Such violins were never meant to be played by ordinary men. But there was nothing to fear since not a single violin was sold anyway.

But none of these violins represented *him*! He had always wanted to make a violin that was a replica of him. One that was neither too emotional nor deep nor too frivolous. Practical perhaps. But one that would capture the essence of his life in its wood and sound box. He wanted to make one Masterpiece that would capture – *truly* capture – his entire life. Like a Diary.

And he was now almost done. He had known it when he touched the blocks his friend had sent. There was something electric in the texture that said to him, "Yes, we will be what you want us to be".

The Violin was almost complete now. He unwrapped it carefully from the cloth and looked at it. It gleamed. It was perfect. It was the perfect violin. He plucked a string timidly. The vibrations came out passionately. And it seemed as though he felt his young wife on his side. He looked, but, of course, she was not there.

Now he lifted his bow and played across the strings. It was as though the heavens had come down to the little cabin. He felt giddy and overwhelmed. He started playing. His fingers took over, as they always did. And music emerged.

And the violin spoke of his childhood, his parents, his grandparents, his school friends, his dogs, his wife, and his children – everyone he had ever met. It remembered tiny incidents that he thought he had forgotten. The room seemed so crowded. People, animals, flowers, books. Everything and everyone he had possibly encountered in his life was in that cabin. The violin changed shape, showing him as a baby, then a young boy, then an adult, then as he was in middle age and finally, it seemed he was seeing himself. His fingers dared not leave the board and kept playing. He went on and on. For hours. Perhaps a whole day.

✦

The wind had finally entered the room, forcing itself in. The door swung on its hinges letting in the icy drafts. Sneering cruelly, the wind chilled everything within the cabin. The Old Man had already gone to the next world, with a soft smile on his face, which rested on the table, cradling his violin, his Masterpiece, like a baby.

But the other children, the violins on the wall, refused to die and they played themselves. Each sang out for its father, thanking him for giving them life. Each wept, knowing that he would never touch them again. Each prayed, in that cabin – no, in that Cathedral – that they would see him again.

18

The Music Feeders

I floated through space listening to this new silence. This silence – this *non-sound* – was different. It was harsh and eerie.

I should explain.

The concert had been bliss. I was sated. Who could understand that our life depended on music? Such a benign existence – our food, that which was needed for our survival, was music. In that we were different. Other formless entities drifted through the curtain of time and space intent on their mission, existing for their own reasons. They fed on energy, blood, light, X-rays – almost anything.

But, we! We fed on music! And we were so placid. Doing nothing to disturb the order of things. Harming no one. We went where there was music, stayed quietly in corners unnoticed, disturbing no one. As notes took shape and came our way, we rested and allowed the notes to enter us, nourishing us, making us feel whole and healthy. And when the music was excellent, the feeling of bliss and complete torpor…we could all recount our own special experiences. The deep emotion in the sustained plaintive note crying out with a sorrow all its own. Lingering, lingering till it died. How much we felt its loss. How well we understood its message. We wondered if the messenger even knew what the message was about. If he did, how could he bear to ignore it? If he could not, how could he express it so beautifully?

Such were our languorous thoughts. We floated from concert to concert. And why only concerts? There was music elsewhere. In the soft whispers of the leaves deep inside jungles. Lovely notes and sounds that only we heard. In the black airless spaces between planets where lost souls roamed restlessly crying out for their partners. Such pain and such melody! We envied them the agony that moved them to create such music!

Deep within oceans where schools of fish dashed madly together in the direction of some deep sublime string of sensuous sounds that erupted randomly and died away rapidly. We moved with them. What a feast for us, and what torture for those we travelled with! Mad with the constant teasing, unable to break away from the quicksand of pure melody. We felt sad – oh so sad, but this was our food! We couldn't live without sound, melody, and harmony!

And there were those amongst us who were addicts. It had to be only *one* kind of music. None else would do. Single minded fanaticism which repelled us, the more civilized forms who appreciated and fed off anything that was melodious –

of course there had to be a certain standard! But the addicts were connoisseurs, with elevated tastes. Specialist gourmands. This music and none other! We pitied them their madness and envied them at the same time.

We watched many of them flitting restlessly listening acutely for that which they needed. There were many that simply had to have music by a Maestro. I loved it too. The contemplative liquid notes, the delicate touch of a rare movement that only he could create – why it was the rare spice that made the difference between a great meal and an excellent one! Yes, those notes hinted at a something, some elusive feeling, and a fleeting flirting with an unknown wisp of emotion. I could understand the hunger and gluttony of the addicts.

Philharmonic addicts, whale symphony addicts, hummingbird addicts. We had all types. For some, nothing but the whispering lilts of falling leaves from certain trees would do. Oh how they suffered! For days they would rush around the earth madly without finding any tree willing to part with its leaves. And then, suddenly, for several days, there would be such a glut of leaves falling that they were in a trance for days afterwards.

As for me, I loved the sounds of the violin. It would drive me mad! I listened to the brilliant delicate tones of Stradivarius violins. I enjoyed the tentative sounds of music from students going through their paces. I curled up inside the sound boxes of many violins and enjoyed the joyous gyrations and melodic avalanches they generated.

But I was equally fond of operatic singers and their deep, throbbing voices. I enjoyed the chants of monks in Tibet. I loved the humming and unexpected twists in the songs at glee clubs. I was swayed by the emotional devotion in the songs of many lands. I loved the Hummingbirds and their laughing trills. Yes, I loved music and was not finicky. It just had to be good. I was not an addict. I knew I had to survive and that music was my food.

And when we rested, it had to be in silence. For which we each had our own little spot in space where we could lie content and undisturbed in soothing silence, digesting what we had taken in.

✦

I could sense that something was coming. The silence had a peculiar shade. We all felt it, and I could see that all of us were looking in the same direction.

Something imploded. We felt the vibration of the moment. For another moment there was stillness and then – something powerful pulled at us. We, made of nothing, were being pulled in to some spot. I tried to escape. I saw the others struggle in vain, desperately trying to escape but the pull was too strong and they were sucked in. I was at a distance and somehow escaped. But yet, I could feel the relentless pull. I was in a panic, not knowing what to do.

When the pull suddenly relaxed, everything around me had changed. Silence had a new hue, an unfamiliar one, strangely harsh and lonely.

I searched for food. There was none. The stars and the planets had ceased to exist. There were no violins. No animals and trees with soft leaves moving beautifully in the wind. No whales singing their tragic melodies.

Nothing.

✦ ✦ ✦

19

One Hundred Seconds of Music

What is this love, I must ask, that flows with the waves of music? What is its promise, what is its appeal, that makes me wipe away in not even a second, that which took a lifetime to create and grow?

The tips of my fingers had touched hers even though I saw her but for a moment.

Lost in my thoughts while listening intently to a moving piece of music, I sat in a bus on my way to wherever I had been forced to go. The sequence of notes said many things and each time something different. And it promised to say something else the next time. I had no choice but to listen to it again and again, that particular 100 second snatch. I looked around and wondered why everyone was oblivious to the glacial and liquid purity of the music I had been fated to listen to.

But how could they? I had on headphones; they had none. They merely heard silence and I – I heard everything.

My heart beat fast and often simply stopped as I tethered on the brink of a precipice of emotion that the music had remorselessly pushed me towards. Why was this music created? Who had thought of the piece? Did he know what it might do to me? Had it happened to him?

On a narrow road, the bus inched forward, snaking ahead slowly. Cycles, people, cattle, other vehicles – all proclaimed, quite violently, their right to exist and move forward. From the other direction came an impossibility – another bus that insisted on occupying the same space as the one in which I travelled. Both buses tried to sneak past each other, dangerously, recklessly. But my eyes were closed, lost as I was in listening to sounds and a sequence that was too absurdly pregnant with meanings that I could not ignore. Meanings I knew that I could not understand and never would. I listened again and again, a film of tears forming and collecting, slowly winding down my cheeks, born without reason and with no destination.

The bus stopped. Through the blur that allowed only a little light and very little comprehension, I saw that the other bus had come to a stop right beside mine. I opened my eyes a little more and saw her look straight at me. She was in the bus opposite, barely six inches away.

She saw me, and she could hear what I was listening to. She knew. She did not need headphones. She blocked out the cacophony just outside, the swearing drivers, the shouts of rage and anxiety. She heard exactly what I was hearing and understood all.

My heart beat with hers, in perfect time and both of us were wafted to the same mystical world that the notes spoke of as they played again and again. Each second was shared. The time and the message were the same.

A vacuum enveloped us shutting out everything, stretching around her, from her window and into mine, and then covering me. In this shell, the sounds of music were shared. We looked at each note, examining it from all angles. Together. Whatever else existed glided past us and away, not wishing to disturb this private pleasure. The notes reverberated, glowing, moving from her eyes to mine. She could hear – but with her eyes. The same movement of notes that brought me ecstatic misery brought glistening tears, as she too understood what I had. In that instant, we knew that we belonged. That the buses had stopped where they had to bring each of our lives to a climax. Those who share music in exactly the same way, love. She might have been deaf, but she had heard. Did it matter that she was on another bus doomed to move away forever within seconds?

Through my closed eyes, shaken by the confluence of heavenly music and love, I saw that she too wept. I knew why. It was the music. It was also the common hatred of what the future would inevitably bring, in only seconds.

The buses pulled away and the vacuum in which we had known each other for an eternity was slowly rent apart. Our hearts stopped. The music had ended too.

Her eyes widened with an appeal as mine might have too. But it was too late.

I could never bring myself to rewind that tape again.

What is this love, I must ask, that flows with the waves of music?

✦ ✦ ✦

20

The Tamarind Tree

Somehow, the wind has changed. The direction, the intensity and the chill – everything has changed. Here it caresses him, there it stabs him. It shrieks insolently about his ears and hums as he breathes and takes in the air.

The ghosts sitting in the tree are wide-awake this blazing afternoon. Not for them the routine of the night. They have waited a very long time for him to come back to his village.

When the letter from his mother reached him, it had seemed that the ink was still fresh. As though she had been in the next room, written the letter and had it sent the very next minute. In the letter, she had announced her impending death in a very firm handwriting. *"I am ill and I have decided to die,"* she had written. *"Now I have only you and after me, you will have no one. It is best if we can meet one last time."* The ink still glistened.

From the Railway station at Kuppam, he had taken the bus to his village. It was a short journey that passed with little incident. No one recognized him. No one had time for a returning son.

In the village, certain things had changed. Most had not. The two huge Banyan trees near the bus stand still watched over the few who transited. The stand had been renovated and the walls whitewashed. A few streetlights conspired to make the place ugly. He walked the short distance to his mother's hut.

Now he is here. The street dogs lie about in shades and bark perfunctorily. They seem to ask, rather resentfully, what his business is. Not as though they were asking a stranger, but rather, a wayward old friend who had not kept his word and done his duty.

Outside the hut, the old family cow still sits with eyes half-closed, her jaws constantly moving, chewing. Does she really chew grass or does she analyze her memories and observations on the human condition? She really knows more about us then we might think, he feels. Unknowingly, we have had a spy watching our home. We have paid no heed to her, quarrelled, and discussed the frailties of our friends and relatives. The cow has sat quietly, ignored by us, listening and taking everything in, processing, processing.

The wind has announced to the world that he has arrived. The leaves of the tamarind tree laugh, but the mango tree seems to hiss. In each leaf is a drop of love for the woman who looked after it since it started its journey upwards, predestined to failure. The tamarind tree gave and gave for her every meal. But she always preferred the mango tree. Had she done the right thing?

His mother's voice still floats about the hut. What a sweet and delicate voice she had, he now thought. While we rushed in and out, demanding our meals, ignoring her every need, she sang and sang old songs. If not for her songs, the food might not have tasted the same; it was that intangible extra spice that went in to the sambar with the tamarind juice.

The walls stood silently, darkened here by the smoke and neglect of years, lightened elsewhere by the filtered sunlight from smudged windows. My Mother! My Mother! They were her silent friends, having absorbed all her music and her silent thoughts. Was she their real mother? Was I related only by blood?

She lies calmly and peacefully on the bed at the far wall. A faint fragrant breeze blows in through the small window near her feet. Many tiny tamarind leaves have spread all over the white bed sheet she had pulled over herself neatly. Her white hair has been neatly combed. She seems to have had a final bath and prayed one last time. The incense sticks has not quite extinguished and the old picture of Rama and Sita with their perennial smiles stands propped up at exactly the place they have been for untold years.

The years of loneliness have finally converged to this day and this time. The son who could not be there while she lived has returned to her a little too late.

Behind him, in his wake, the air has stilled and rested on the hard brown road.

The ghosts have noted the event in their diaries. They will return to haunt with a vengeance. The sparrows have returned earlier than usual and rest quietly on the branches on the mango tree. The crows watch him discretely from the other tree.

Is that where her soul has gone to rest?

21

Philosophy for Fools

A Book Review
Penguin & Peacock Publishers
I had been waiting for quite a while to get my hands on this remarkable non-book, written by me.

I knew I had surpassed my own inanity but I needed to confirm it. So, when I was sent a complimentary copy and asked to review it, I grabbed at the opportunity, wanting to sink my teeth into something amazingly bad and rotten.

Where does one begin? At the beginning. I raise, inanely, the query "What is Truth?" I meander in different directions, speaking vaguely of God, Indira Gandhi, Ronald Reagan, coffee planters in El Salvador, rice-growers in Okinawa and on and on and I never get to the point, until I suddenly say "And that, my friends, is the Truth". Eh? How ridiculous is that?

Read this appalling nonsense written by me:

"A philosophical detachment, one hesitates to say, is needed by Pizza lovers, surrounded by ghoulish ads and coupons, delivery

options, five pizzas for the price of six or six pizzas for the price of one. When will this madness end?"

When indeed. Judging by my extraordinary ability to generate certified nonsense, the end is not near. No, indeed. And for that you and I must pay the price.

In the middle are some entirely irrelevant pictures and graphics of Lake Titicaca and a laughing Lama (the animal), a photo of Michaelangelo eating broccoli and one of a sleeping dog, sleeping. There are no captions. The pictures are just – there. There is no reference to them anywhere. How this helps in the progression of the book is something that mystifies me, and in fact, if I recall, it mystified me even when I wrote it. But no, I just had to insert them there.

Suddenly, the "author", VM (I, me, myself), raises the penetrating but completely irrelevant question "Should Tuesdays be moved immediately after Friday?". He obviously assumes that the reader is a fool (admittedly, the title says so too), but when he challenges me (the author himself), one simply does reverse cartwheels in a bid to hold on to a wisp of sanity. Is this question one of philosophy? That's what VM would have us believe.

The bizarreness of the book includes pages that are numbered out of sequence, some that are printed in landscape mode for no obvious reason, some pages in art paper and some in regular GSM, some pages completely blank (with a foolish blurb *"This page has been left intentionally blank"*) and so on. The Preface is at the end. The last chapter is in the middle. The Foreword is claimed to be by Kofi Annan, the UN Secretary General, and he makes the claim that this book is fantastic and will always be remembered for uniting the world. On recollection, I now see that he meant that the world would be united in seeking to impale the author (me) to a cardboard sheet like a lepidopterist might do to a moth.

The saving grace of this book is that it actually does end. I breathed a sigh of relief. In the book, I have promised to write another book called "Dogs and Cats – Philosophical Confabulations". I sincerely hope I will not write the book, but knowing myself, I think I will. Heaven help me and the readership.

22

The Lama

With grateful thanks to Herma Caelen, Brussels. And details checked personally on a couple of trips to Brussels.

"I shall be dead in 15 minutes," said the Lama softly, in quiet, unaccented English.

"Oh really?" I chuckled. "You look pretty good to me."

I yawned and stretched. Night shift was always a pain. After all these years, I still hadn't adjusted, but I had to do what I had to do. Which came with being an Inspector at one of Brussels police stations.

I glanced across the table and at the far wall where the Lama sat, erect and comfortable on the bench. I puffed at my cigarette and examined him through the smoke as I exhaled slowly.

"How old is he, I wonder," I thought to myself. "Unusual guy. Doesn't seem like a nut but who can tell…."

I sipped my coffee. It was tasteless. And it had no sugar at all.

"We know," said the Lama suddenly.

"We?" I asked, blowing rings lazily. It was one at night and I was bored. A little small talk with a detainee would help while passing time.

"You and I. We know." said the Lama, closing his eyes and smiling very softly.

"Know what?" I asked, genuinely puzzled.

He did not reply.

For the briefest of moments, my heart stopped. Something within me agreed. Something within me said, "Yes, I know". I was overwhelmed.

His eyes opened and he smiled.

"Don't be afraid," he said, without opening his mouth or making any sound. His purple robes suddenly seemed a shade red.

"Me!? Afraid!? Don't play games with me!" I suddenly shouted, sitting up straight in my chair.

"Paul!" I shouted, "Paul! Come here, please!"

The duty constable rushed in, alarmed. I rarely shouted.

"What's wrong with this coffee? There's no taste at all! Did you change something? Maybe it needs more sugar!" I was quite agitated.

Paul looked puzzled.

"But Sir, you put in two spoons in my presence yourself! And we haven't changed the coffee!"

"Can you please get more sugar? I need to have a chat with our friend here. This may take some time."

"At once, Sir!" said Paul and rushed out.

A moment later, he was back with a bowl of sugar and I helped myself to two more spoonfuls. In fact, three more. My hand was trembling noticeably.

Paul retreated with the bowl, with a puzzled look on his face, glancing at the Lama and then me. I knew what he would tell his friends tomorrow. "Inspector Vermeersch...."

"There is very little time, my son," said the Lama suddenly in a quiet voice.

"For what?" I asked angrily. I couldn't understand why this Asian vagabond was causing me to lose my cool. And why were his robes appearing a darker red than before?

"The time is coming," he whispered, very softly, hardly moving his lips.

"Shut up!" I roared angrily. "I'll show you whose time has come! Now better start explaining what you were doing with all those dogs."

I had received three calls that evening. One was from the Mayor himself and the others from two respected citizens. There was this strange Tibetan Lama walking across the Grand Place. Following him were more than forty dogs of every shape and size.

But what struck everyone was this: All the dogs were following the Lama silently.

It was the strangest procession anyone had ever seen, in the heart of Brussels.

The Mayor was worried; election time was near, the city ought to be free of weirdoes and stray animals. Yes Sir, I said.

"Obviously some kind of trouble-maker or nut, I had better check him out", I thought, and went with Paul to investigate, as it came within my precinct.

When I saw him, the Lama was seated on a bench, with his eyes closed, with some beads in his fingers, which he was constantly shifting between his thumb and forefinger. There was not a soul anywhere near.

Which too was odd.

And all the dogs were sitting quietly, with no sound from any of them. Not a whine or a bark. Nothing.

Of course, since I liked dogs, I didn't drive them away. I walked up to the Lama and asked him to accompany me. He did so, without resistance.

And the dogs followed, silently.

Paul and I looked at each other. We decided, inexplicably, to ignore them. We walked into the Police Station and the dogs stayed outside, very obediently.

✦

The Lama did not answer.

"This sugar is useless", I roared in frustration. Paul opened the door and peeped in.

"Anything wrong, Sir?"

"I need more Sugar! The coffee is still bitter! Something is really wrong, Paul!"

"Yes Sir," said Paul, hurriedly, and rushed in with the whole bowl. I helped myself to four more spoons. Paul looked worried. But he knew better than to say anything.

As Paul departed, I looked again at the Lama.

His robes were now blood red.

"Must see the doctor tomorrow," I made a note to myself.

"The Soul is ready to leave. Do you feel it?" asked the Lama, in very soft tones.

Somehow, I felt it. My head was swimming. Me, a Police Inspector in the heart of Europe, involved in some strange metaphysical dialogue with a Lama from Tibet.

I became aware of a strange throbbing sound. It had seemed to be there for a while. It was just louder now.

Some rock concert nearby, I thought irritably. Or a car with loudspeakers. At this time of night. Idiots.

"Paul!" I shouted, "Where's that damned sound coming from?"

"Let me check, Sir", he said, and stepped out.

Then he ran back in.

"You had better see this Sir", he said, his face ashen. There was a distinct tremor in his voice.

Frowning, I stood up and followed Paul to the window near his desk and looked out.

All the dogs were lined up, five to a row.

The throbbing sound, like an eerie chant, was coming from them.

And I, who had never crossed the borders of Belgium, *knew that chant and knew what it meant!*

And in the darkness, the reflected red light outside the Police Station, falling on the dogs, gave the amazing impression that they were wearing robes. Just like the Lama.

And with exactly the same red colour.

Paul and I shrank back from the window.

We rushed to the room.

Silent and powerful gusts were sweeping across the room. Papers were flying from end to end. My coffee cup was rattling softly in the saucer. The Lama was sitting quietly in the same place where I had left him.

Papers swirled around him and I could almost sense that everything was being pulled in. To him. A light enveloped the Lama and the chanting became louder and louder. And was sucked into him.

The Lama's eyes opened and fixed themselves on mine. And at that moment, I *knew*. I just *knew*.

He gave me everything.

And, just as suddenly as it had started, the gusts subsided.

As Paul and I watched, the Lama literally dissolved into thin air, ever so slowly.

Outside, the chanting from the dogs had stopped.

I rushed to the window and looked down.

The Dogs had vanished too.

23

Confessions of a Former Writer

I happened to emerge from yet another night at the Police Station where I had been interrogated by unfriendly policemen for the usual crime. The neighbours had been complaining that I had been writing and they couldn't tolerate the nuisance and the bad influence on children, adults and pet piranha in aquaria.

"Back again?" sighed the Sub-Inspector. "You Sir, are a menace to society." He knew me well. A nuisance writer, an intolerable presence in a quiet conservative neighbourhood with only the occasional murder or two.

I stood with head bent, gazing down at my tattered socks and shoes, my toes peeping out timidly. Silence is always wise.

"Why do you write?" he asked, and my head jerked up as I thought I detected a tone of sympathy in his voice.

I blabbered like a fool "*...from my heart... life experiences... because I must... because it's there... Feelings... Emotions... Sentiments... Creating... Posterity...*"

A grave mistake. The Police Inspector nodded at someone behind me. I was beaten up. Extremely well. By a classy new police recruit. I made a note to write a note about modern techniques in beatings.

So, as I was saying, I staggered out. My limbs were broken but my proud heart was unbowed.

I crawled into a building where I saw a board saying "Inter-University English Professors Conference to discuss the fall in writing standards". Here I would be fed and vaccinated and given a warm bed, I thought.

I bribed my way in. I attended an interview with the Chief Server of Refreshments and he appointed me 'Head of Horse Devours', whatever that meant. Inside were several English Professors standing in lewd positions, discussing dead writers and second-hand books.

A gorgeous old thing, sleeveless blouse, elaborate backside, a Professor of English from Delhi was speaking: "...a Dickensonian perspective on the writings of Mohammad Ababba...post-colonialism...pre-Victorian... I just loved your critique of the character of his homosexual parrot...." She picked up a samosa from my silently proffered plate and ate it, whole, in one large movement. I saw the samosa peep out at me, begging to be saved. Then, it was gone. Forever. A silent scream, unheard.

An old English Professor covered with cobwebs from Calcutta University: "...insufferable language. If you ask me, Yeats has been overrated. I've been saying this for years, but you know how political these poets are. My personal preference is Edward Fontainebleau, the Angle-French poet and his capitalized poems: IN A RESTAURANT, DEATH, LIFE, POST OFFICE... people just don't know how to read capitalized poems anymore, the way education has deteriorated...."

He picked up two samosas, placed one in his pocket for later examination and ate the other in three exquisite bites, which I still remember with a shiver; it was so artistic. I walked away, benumbed by the genius I had seen

"I...I...I've just joined University of F___ as a Lecturer," stammered an insipid middle-aged man, introducing himself to a woman with a magnificent bust, clearly the Queen of Literary Criticism.

"Indeed?" said the Doyenne, regally. "How many years? Topic?"

"Fifteen. My topic was a study of your criticisms of other literary criticisms."

The lady softened. "Ah, finally. I must see a copy of your dissertation. I must say though, that fifteen years working on your PhD seems rather brief. In my time," – here she shook her head in disdain, remembering her hoary and hairy past when she had been a svelte young thing with a mean and acerbic pen that could destroy the futures of dead poets – "Twenty years was a reasonable time to work on a Doctorate." Her admirers broke into a collective wailing and chest-beating (their own) about the fall in standards.

They saw me standing at the periphery respectfully with a plateful of samosas. They saw that I was lean and hungry. They took away all the samosas and ate them. "What do you do?" asked the lady with the bust and the doctorate, absently, chomping away.

"Uh, I write".

A deathly silence fell on the august assembly. A shiver of menace, a miasma, a cold wind, the howls of wolves.

The new lecturer broke into hysterical maniacal laughter and was slapped by other lecturers to bring him to his senses. Elsewhere, I heard an English Lecturer from Oxford retch; it had been too much to bear.

"What do you think you're doing here?" asked a tall muscular gentleman with an unfriendly literary twist in his tone. He was obviously a Doctoral student. "You Sir, are a menace to society!"

A feeling of deja vu descended. Where had I heard those words before?

"I thought English Professors would encourage writers," I whispered feebly in self-defense. "I thought you were writers yourself."

It was the last straw. It was absolutely the wrong thing to say.

Uneaten samosas, lukewarm tea, work-in-progress, critical reviews of work written hundreds of years ago, discarded dissertations – all rained down on me. I do not recall greater physical and mental pain.

I heard a confused babble of voices, shrill shrieks of outrage and more.

"How dare a writer infiltrate?"

"How dare he write?"

"What gall! To insinuate that we might be *writers*!"

The Chief Server of Refreshments rushed in, dismissed me summarily from my position of Head of Horse Devours and personally escorted me out with a sharp kick to my posterior.

I walked home slowly, solemn, chastened. Stray dogs barked at me. Unfriendly crows dove down from trees to peck at me. Urchins pointed and mouthed abuses. As I staggered into the lane where I lived, I heard muffled screams and doors being slammed.

Yes, I said, yes. The answer was obvious.

I took out reams of short stories and manuscripts, poems and drafts. I dumped them in the middle of the lane. I sprinkled kerosene on the pile.

Neighbours had started collecting, curious to know what I might be doing.

I lit a match and threw it in the heap. The pile burst into flames, putting the sun to shame.

A great cry of joy went up from my neighbours, who I had tortured so thoughtlessly for so long. Housewives wept. Ancient old men fingered prayer beads, muttering praises to the Gods. Dogs finally wagged their atrophied tails. Children rushed to me and hugged my legs, knowing that there was now a chance for them to regain their innocence.

It had been worth it.

24

Poetry Outsourcing – a True Tale

It was a dark and stormy evening.

KK, Smoky and I (names changed for their safety) had agreed to meet at Verses, an arty restaurant in downtown Bangalore, ostensibly to discuss Recent Trends in Poetry and how WTO would impact Deep Thoughts.

KK was quiet. Smoky was not. I listened to a dull throbbing in the air.

"You are now a Poet. There are secrets that you must know," said KK, puffing on his cigarette. Here he broke into a Sonnet, which I am unable to repeat due to its sensitive and confidential nature. I bent down to touch the feet of this Master.

Smoky at this point spoke about Transcendental Meditation, Processes and what a time he had in Delhi.

"Are you ready for the Truth?" said the mystic (KK) in front of me, his eyes penetrating my very soul.

"Yes," I said calmly, "yes".

And I knew I was.

Smoky spoke well now about snake catching, vacuums in life and so forth. He lit a cigarette.

KK snapped his fingers. A man in spotless white appeared. He was a waiter. KK nodded at him. We rose from the table and went into the bowels of Verses. He took us past revolving doors and behind the oven. A new world opened up.

"This is the Poetry Center. This is deadly serious business, and I mean it," whispered KK. "Let's take a walk around. Poetry is now big business and this is the place where deals are cut, careers built and ruined. Since you are now a Poet, you must know what's really going on."

First, several large and beefy Chinese with slick hair body-searched us. "Security Risk. No poems allowed," said KK in Tamil to me.

A Guide joined us and shook our hands, crushing my fingers.

"I'm Chang and I'll be your guide tonight. You're in the Global Ops center. You can say that this is the world's poetry marketplace. If a poem wasn't bought or sold here, it has no value. Stick close to me if you value your life."

I was impressed. "Is it stressful?" I asked.

"Not if you know what you're doing," said Chang, with a light laugh. "We make sure we have the highest quality of poets and poems here. Take a look at those guys in black suits and bow ties and dark glasses walking around with walkie-talkies. They know when something's going wrong."

At this point, Smoky lamented the falling standards of Journalism. He asked questions about healthcare for which we had no answer, as we were taking in the scene. He lit a cigarette.

At every table, poets were engaged. At one, a young man, thin, blood-red eyes, shivering with soul-fever, stood up, making a presentation to three suited businessmen from Mumbai, who listened impassively. "Three poems on Love," he muttered, "Fifty words each, I can't do more. Please. I don't have health insurance." The businessmen shook their heads as one, impassively. "Five and Eighty, or no deal." The young man wept. We walked on, eyes averted. The pain was more than we could bear. We felt we had intruded in someone's personal space.

Smoky asked if I had met Mahatma Gandhi. No, I said. Me neither, he responded, and laughed hysterically. He lit a cigarette.

At another table, a large one, an array of Japanese listened carefully to their leader. "Outsourcing. Haiku. We try. How many? How much you can write?"

A young girl with big eyes, three nose rings and a green silk sari responded in flawless Japanese, the essence of which was that her poetry company could develop about 75 haikus in a month, give or take a dozen, and she would charge 1 rupee per.

"You produce 400 per month, we pay 80 paise per haiku. Productivity not good. Demand high. Quality must improve. We see how you maintain. Maybe later, we increase," said the man from Tokyo. The deal was struck.

Smoky inquired if I liked Bhajans and Hymns. I said yes. He lit a cigarette.

Further away, an American delegation with laptops and Cowboy Boots laughed uproariously, as the company they wanted to outsource poetry composition to make a presentation.

"You call *that* a poem!?" chuckled their Leader, named Johnson. "Yo Man! Even your Poem has an accent! Ha ha ha ha!"

The Indian did not take the bait. "It is up to you. We have quality processes and insist that every sixth poem uses the word "mist". We have 24 x 7 connectivity and we whip our poets four times a day. You'll save on 50% of your costs."

"Do you edit?" asked Johnson.

The Indian gave him a withering look. "Poets don't edit," he said. The menace in his voice was unmistakable.

Johnson looked embarrassed. "Of course, of course," he said hurriedly. "No offence, OK Man, this is cool, let's do it. Fifty cents per poem. 2000 poems per month. Minimum length 34 words. We send topics. You write. You'll need to sign an NDA. We'll need resumes."

"Naturally," said the Indian, scornfully. "We've moved up the value chain."

Here, the air was punctured by a scream. We turned. Chang's friends were hauling away another thin wild-eyed poet with an attitude and a goatee. No one else turned a hair.

"He's an incompetent poet," Chang explained. "There are rules. He will die."

Smoky asked, "What was his crime?"

"He wrote poems that rhymed," said Chang, blandly.

I turned pale. Just recently, I had been trying to find a word that rhymed with 'cockroach'.

Smoky lit a cigarette. KK stroked his beard thoughtfully.

We moved towards the exit. "Those are the dungeons on the right," said Chang, with another light laugh. We heard low moans, weeping, high-pitched screams and snaps of whips. We didn't have to say anything. We knew. These were failed poets, condemned forever. Wasted careers, wasted lives. But it was a choice they had made.

We walked up the stairs and out on to the main road. A girl with a white cat in her arms brushed past us in the opposite direction and hurried away. Outside, the world carried on, oblivious of the goings-on in that building. We shook hands. Smoky lit a cigarette with trembling hands. We each turned and walked away into our own sunsets. I was tempted to write a poem, but I controlled myself.

25

Soul Food

If you like being frightened by things like blood and gore, then you should not read further. That is because this tale does not have these tedious elements in them, and you will not find what you are looking for.

The material world remains fundamentally the same, offering little in terms of excitement to one who seeks to swim in the occult, where grim menace emerges unexpectedly, where horror is subtle and not stretched in time, or grotesquely sprinkled with the intent to unsettle and disturb. In the occult world that I visit, horror is permanent and accepted and has no connotation of evil. It is merely – and correctly – another aspect of the universe and does not come with childish and naïve labels like 'good' or 'evil'. The very word 'horror' is inadequate and is an application of a tedious, contrived value system that refers to some kind of dissonance or an excitement of our nerves in a certain way. With horror comes the feeling of being extinguished in a manner not of one's choosing. And that then is how it actually is.

After death, you see, our souls are herded together, like so many cattle and we are yoked and taken to a point near the star Procyon of the Canis Minor constellation, where we are cleansed and examined for any defects and sorted. We, as those previously alive, but still with a glimmering of understanding of a sense of self, are put through a sieve of sorts and certified.

For what, you ask, perhaps anxiously. Well, my dear Sir or Madam, we are truly soul food, intended for consumption by a more powerful entity, a genuinely permanent reality that needs to eat and stay alive for purposes beyond explanation. Preposterous, you say? It does not matter. Your experiences, while you lived, actually do season your soul and give it an extra spice, which makes for gourmet consumption. And so, near Procyon, your soul is sorted and accumulated in one of many little bottles depending on the hue your life took. Later, your last sense of self is extinguished as you are consumed, yes indeed.

You protest and say that you lived a good life? I applaud you, but regret to say it merely means you shall be used as an ingredient, no less, no more. Were you shockingly evil and did you deliberately cause pain and suffering? It does not matter. You too shall be used for food. Perhaps this causes bitter disappointment, setting your value systems on their head. Perhaps you are frightened, not of death any longer, but the lingering endless waiting of your soul in a container as you wait your turn to be picked up and eaten. *That* extinguishing, *that* event – now *that* will truly be death.

I see that the innocent, the good, the evil, the macabre, the cruel, the soft and compassionate are all equal and are merely crops of different varieties. Each is allowed to grow till it is ready for harvesting. Then arrives the state we call physical death, where the soul is extracted and taken to Procyon as described.

This journey requires telling. The first step, immediately after physical death, involves setting free the soul. It is extracted from the top of the head and immediately chained and constrained. You will be bewildered and confused. How different this is from just a few moments ago, you will wonder. Your dignity is stripped and you are tied to other similarly newly-dead with ropes of ether. Not knowing what else you could possibly do in this bodyless state, you will be in a state of stupor, completely terrified, uncomprehending, wondering what next.

And soon there will be a tug and you will hopelessly drift in the direction of Procyon, which you may not even have known existed, except in distorted ways in books here and there. By now you would have realized that you are being manipulated against your will, what little there still is of it. But you cannot protest, for you know not how to express this feeling and you know not who could listen and what they could possibly do. But *fright* overwhelms you, as you sense a complete and final loss of control. You are truly paralyzed.

And now at Procyon, you sense many such agglomerations of similarly baffled souls who seek pointless freedom of a sort. The sense of darkness is overwhelming. You are roughly handled and dipped through a soup of what seems purple fire, but which is in fact a kind of cleansing pool. You will emerge, washed but yet completely helpless. You will be separated and herded, based on some criteria which you cannot understand and then placed with millions of similar entities. Now your sense of time will leave you. You have nothing to look forward to and have no idea how to mark the passage of time and what to do about it. So you wait, awake for eternities, completely subjugated, completely removed of dignity and respect, for these mean nothing any longer. Were you once compassionate to a sick puppy? Did you once kill an old helpless lady? Neither means anything here – they merely added a kind of spice to your soul and made it additionally attractive for consumption.

And then the Event will unfold. You will be pulled out, helpless, paralyzed, uncomprehending. And you shall feel that sense of being consumed.

That will be the final darkness.

26

Flight NA100 to Mumbai

I knew I would never see him again, but I did not speak out. As the Captain and Pilot of Night Air 100, my duties do not include needless chatter with passengers.

The taxi dropped me at the airport at about 1 a.m. and I walked past the security personnel, who ignored me completely, as though I did not exist. The place was quiet and deserted. I walked through the final doors and then on the tarmac towards my plane, a Boeing 737 waiting motionlessly in a dark area of the airport, very far away from the terminal. It stood silently, blacker than night, glowing with tales and mystery. Not a soul was around. I got into the cockpit and started up the engines and went through the manifest and papers. I went through the checks and let the engine idle and waited for my passengers. I turned on the lights in the cockpit. Then I looked into the blackness and waited. And waited. I had all the time in the world.

And soon I saw him, my lone passenger, running across the large concrete expanse, breathless, with two small bags in his hands. I waved at him from the cockpit window and saw the relief on his face from a distance. He clambered on, huffing and puffing, a short fat businessman.

He peeped into the cockpit. "NA 100 to Mumbai?" he asked, gasping, trying to catch his breath. I nodded, not turning around.

He went to find his seat, and then returned a moment later.

"No air hostess? No other passengers?" he asked, a moment later, a bit nervously.

"Nope. It's just us. One Pilot. One passenger. It happens sometimes. Red-eye flight, you know."

"Ah."

"We're ready to go. Please sit down and fasten your seat belt."

"Of course, of course," he said hurriedly. In the mirror, I saw him turn and walk back quickly to his assigned seat. A fat businessman on a mission to make more and more money. I shut the door to the cockpit, made the routine announcements on the intercom and dimmed the lights. It was pitch dark now, inside and outside.

I taxied the plane to the head of the runway and announced an imminent takeoff. The lights were off on the runway too, but I knew the way, having taken off so often. I revved the engines and gathered speed. Faster, faster, faster. The plane shook, trembled and rattled as it trundled down the runway, against the wind, about to lift off, about to take off into the black moonless night, about to take my passenger to his destination.

And soon it took off. A sleek black arrow with one pilot and one passenger. I angled the plane up and away, seeking to gain height as much as possible.

Then I saw it, once again, another 737 right in my flight path. Where had it emerged from? Why hadn't I been warned?

And my plane crashed straight into the other plane and we went up in flames together, lighting up the night.

I had failed in my task to take my passenger to Mumbai. Perhaps another hundred passengers in the other plane had also died.

Tonight I am scheduled to fly NA100 once again to Mumbai. At the same time. From the same place.

I wonder who my passenger will be.

27

The Tanpura

Whenever she lifted the Tanpura, the Raags within stirred in their sleep.

No matter how long it had been since she last selected one of them, everyone felt the same excitement. How beautiful she was! They couldn't see her of course, but they knew. And they really meant her heart and the absolute purity that was obvious. There was none better or more ideal for them to reveal themselves to in their complete nakedness. They longed to tell her all their secrets. And they knew that she knew secrets about them that they had no idea about.

In fact, if they had known, she was as beautiful in form. The perfect woman. Gentleness and compassion in her eyes, and oh those eyes! Those eyes! Longing, love, compassion, softness – the perfect woman, completely devoid of anger, completely disinterested in herself.

She caressed the strings and brought them into harmony, perfectly tuned. The strings gave themselves to her, anxious to be corrected, anxious to please. They knew she knew what to do. This was not the time to assert themselves separately, but to hold each other and create the tapestry she wanted.

The wood glowed inwardly, at once proud and humble, that she had chosen it to invoke her God through the music that was still to be born. It was the vehicle and it knew what it had to do. As she strummed the strings the wood caught each note, examined it and removed every imperfection, added its own blessing and released it for the universe to enjoy.

The pegs turned as she asked them and swore to stay firm even if they themselves swayed to the magic of her music and lost their grip from time to time. They knew how important it was to stay firm, and not disturb her concentration.

The air stopped, breathless, waiting for her to sing. Or to hum.

Each Raag tried respectfully and tremulously to invade her mind and make her select him or her. Her eyelids closed, like petals, and her forehead cleared. Her throat gently vibrated, deciding what to sing, how to sing, how loudly and with what emotion. Would it be a note alone in its own glorious splendour? Or would it be a few of them, strung together like a necklace of pearls? No one knew. No one ever knew.

With the greatest of love, she selected one almost at random telling the others lovingly that their turn too would come. Satisfied that she remembered them, the others stepped back and listened carefully to their sibling in its moment of a lifetime. They were not jealous; they prayed that it should seize this chance and immortalize itself, expressing itself through this most just of women.

And so she would sing, eyes closed, plucking the Tanpura in her little prayer room and asking the Raag to carry her thoughts to her God. She blessed the Raag, which in turn blessed her. The Raag gave itself to her completely, leaving nothing hidden. None of the notes gave anything but their best. When each emerged, they waited with excitement for the next and sighed with tremulous excitement and contentment that it too was born, perfect in itself and perfect in relation to what came before and after.

The Raag sighed in ecstasy, completely revealing itself, its vibrations merging with the cosmos, immortal and traveling forever in every direction. She was possessed with devotion. And she would choose the right Raag. Was it a gentle rebuke to God for not helping someone who she knew needed him? Or was it an affectionate missive to tell Him that she had thought of Him? Or was it the mother in her, gathering the Raags around her and sprinkling love on them, reminding them of who they were?

28

The Madness of Music

I shall now tell you the tale of a boy consumed by music. Such a possession is only for the gifted and blessed. They are not to live a normal life. They cannot interact with others in a certain predictable manner. For them, the only thing that makes sense is silence and music.

At exactly the moment he came into being, the madness started.

He grew up slowly, uncomprehending. Sounds kept sloshing around in his head like water in a bucket. But all the sounds made sense. None were really random. All were beautiful; all were logical and yet defied logic. He was a creature of music.

Childhood was so difficult. He saw no need for speech, as he was too busy listening, too busy lost in the rapture of music being born spontaneously, for internal consumption only. His family first found it amusing, then exasperating and then maddening. Who had the time to look after an idle body with eyes that looked far away, completely disinterested in everyday life and relationships? His limbs were always jerking in rhythms all their own, while he babbled incoherently.

Quite by chance, they found that the only way to calm him was to play soothing music. It could be anything – devotional, romantic or relaxing. But it had to be music. No one knew anything about music in his family. The harsh business of life made the appreciation of music appear an idle pastime for the rich and vulgar. They felt cursed that someone in their family should have been born with such a disease.

Only his father was sympathetic. He took his silent son with him on the handlebar of his cycle to his shop in the middle of the tiny town where they lived. He fed him, he cleaned him and he helped with his clothes. He was rough with him but only sometimes when he saw that others expected him to. No one had time to spare for a mad little boy who was lost in his musical thoughts.

His father thought that by being in the shop all day, he might slowly mature and learn how to make a living. But the boy was not interested. His eyes were vacant but something inside danced furtively and often darted from side to side. Often only the whites of his eyes were visible and both his hands were raised upright, bent at the elbows and frozen and disturbed only by random jerks. When it became a disturbance, his father was forced to leave him at a nearby temple, which the boy seemed to like because someone was always singing. Of course, he had to chain him, much against his heart. Otherwise the boy might wander off and get lost.

When his father lifted him, often with moist eyes, telling him that they had to go here or there, the boy crooned and hummed. He liked this person though he had no idea of the formal connection between them.

Even to his father's unsophisticated ears, the genius was unmistakable. Snatches of lovely tunes suddenly burst forth from his son for only a few seconds at a time. His father felt sorry for himself that he did not know enough to capture those tunes forever.

And those headaches, oh those headaches! He held his head tightly between his hands and rocked back and forth. Soundlessly sometimes and sometimes accompanied by tunes of extreme pain. The only remedy was more music from the outside. He would then raise his head slowly, and sometimes smile. But not before his father saw the strands of pain across his face slowly melting away. At such times his father stood still, deeply moved, realizing that his son had been born to the wrong family, at the wrong time. Yes, perhaps he should not have been born at all.

His own mother, a practical woman, had no time for him, busy as she was with the other children. His brothers and sisters ignored him or teased him. Soon they got bored and let him crawl around. He learnt how to get out of their way as he got older and hid under his father's bed, holding his father's shirt close and rocking back and forth. Sometimes, the sounds in his head were too loud. Sometimes, they were so soft and teasing. When that happened, he would hunt for them feverishly in his head. They were always elusive, disappearing around the corner just as he thought he had pounced on them.

And that search would take its toll on his body and he would slither under the bed randomly. In the beginning the other children would peep under the bed and laugh and giggle at the silly sight. Then they lost interest.

As time relentlessly moved on, events took place that he had no idea about. What did time mean anyway? Along the way his dear father died. His mother and his grown brothers took firm decisions and abandoned him overnight at the temple, which he used to like. The priest saw that the boy (Boy? he was now almost twenty!) had some peculiar spiritual insights that did not lend themselves to verbal expression. He allowed him to stay at the temple and was able to put him into a soothing routine where he cleaned the temple floors again and again hour after hour. The gleaming tiles seemed to make the boy happy and his tunes were more lilting than ever before. Never repeated, never waiting to be written. The Goddess, whose temple it was, smiled on benignly and indulgently. The priest allowed him to sleep in the inner room with the idol – in fact that was the only enclosed space available. For the boy's own safety, the priest locked him up at the end of the day and returned home.

Every morning, when the priest opened the door, he could sense vibrations. The boy was asleep, huddled with his thumb in his mouth, and the idol was intact. There must have been music, he knew, but respect kept him from investigating further. There was divine worship of a different kind, he inferred humbly, and he was not privy to that. That is the way it ought to be.

But the next priest was not so insightful or compassionate. The temple had become famous for its gleaming interiors and throbbing energy. A couple of coincidences and ecstatic devotees later, people were only too ready to believe that wishes were granted if one prayed for a child or for wealth. And who can fight fervent devotion?

Soon, the priest grew tired of the mad boy. "Why", he wondered, "is it necessary for this boy to be here? He takes up space, he eats, and I have to spend money on him. Why should I?" And so one night he took him by bullock-cart on a highway and threw him out at a lonely spot about fifteen kilometers away.

As he correctly guessed, it made no difference to the devotees, who continued to flock to the temple and make lavish donations to the deity. He and they did not know that the Goddess had also fled, to be with the boy.

And what of the boy? In the beginning, his dulled nerves moved restlessly for a while and a mild sensation of fear crept through his being, as he tried to understand what was going on. But very soon, it made no difference and he continued to hum and wander about aimlessly. He walked into a village nearby by chance, where the children shouted at him and yelled that a mad boy had come. A few threw stones, which hurt, but he was too far away in a different dimension to really care. He kept walking endlessly, changing directions at random, and not responding to abuses or any kind of question. But it happened that he was somehow always at the periphery of this village.

And one day, he sat under a tree a little away from the village, his body suddenly quite tired. It was hunger, but how was he to know what to do about it. He had eaten nothing for an entire week. He lay down and fell asleep.

He woke up at about 3 am, perhaps racked by stomach pangs. Stars twinkled in the dark blue night above and the leaves in the tree rustled gently. The air was cool and there was no other sound. It was a peaceful tranquil moment.

But who was this lady sitting quietly by him? She had taken his head in her lap and was smiling softly and humming a tune. Of course he knew that tune! And as he thought of the next tune that was in his mind, she sang the same. How comforting! How interesting! His mind kept leaping from tune to tune and this wonderful woman picked it up and finished it for him. Here, finally, was someone who understood him!

Now all the music that he had ever had in his head came gushing out, to be matched and amplified by this most wonderful woman, who never stopped smiling. His ecstasy knew no bounds; happiness made him shudder and gurgle. Paroxysms of joy threatened to rip him apart. His soul had found that one person who understood him and knew what to do, who knew what he was all about.

At dawn, a farmer on his way to his field stumbled upon the still-warm body of the boy.

The farmer remarked to his friends that he had never seen a smile of such pure joy on the face of someone dead.

29

The Man from Jizan

by Sami al-Mutlaq[1]

I had walked along the coast from Jizan, where I lived in loneliness, surrounded by those who loved me, but to whom I could display no feeling. My heart was heavy, I knew not why, and I sought solitude and time to think of nothing. Not for me the hysterics of human form, of predictable acts and experiences, of empty conversations. I sought release and the beauty of solitude and my own company.

And so I left one night, while my children were lost in their dreams and my wife dreamed of our children sleeping next to her. The moon was full, and the stars shone down, witness to the silent swoops of majestic owls searching for shattered and discarded pieces of love. But I walked with head bowed, looking at the approaching sand on which my feet were to

1 a pseudonym used by the author

tread, with no thought in mind except to escape from peace and innocence. I took my Oud with me, for only music could touch my soul and truly understand.

Along the coast of the Red Sea, the waters lapped at my feet, pleaded with me to stay and to return, for my young children had woken up and asked for their father, and their mother answered in a cracked voice that he had gone away and would perhaps return or perhaps not. The waters had heard their sobs and wept for them. But I was deaf and wished to hear only the silence of the mountains and the contemptuous mocking of the crickets.

In Jeddah, I chanced upon old friends. They looked away, for the desert winds had carried the tale of my cruel act to their ears and they had wept for my children. But they gave me dates in silence, and their prayers. I carried on to the north and to Hejaz and soon the chatter of mankind dimmed and I was truly with nature, anonymous, insignificant, free of the bonds of family, believing that such love was merely transient and selfish, and that true everlasting love dwelt on the undulations of mountains.

The towering cliffs, the pure rocks, the trees with roots lurching into the sky, the wild grass protecting the small yellow flowers...these are the blessings of Allah, not wealth, not the desires of a brief lifetime.

And when men labour to climb the lonely narrow paths through the hills, they bring inconsequence. I did too and I knew I had no value, but I climbed up and up, watching the majestic eagles that ignored me. The squirrels too looked up but once and went away, ignoring the face of sin. It seemed that the flowers too looked at me and then turned away, finding purity in the blue sky. I looked below and saw the endless desert where I might choose to become sand too. But I sat on a ledge near the trees, accepting that I was human and superior only in my delusional mind.

I sat there silently, for hours, for days, shrinking within, understanding more and more that I could never be part of such wonder. I had nothing to offer. I would be dust. But the rocks and the eagles and the wind would remain.

I lifted the Oud and offered it to the heavens. Then I played gently, only one note and then another. My fingers caressed the strings, asking them to reveal their beautiful secrets. And I played as I had never played before, as the spirits of the mountains entered me and twisted my fingers as they pleased and brought out that music which had never been heard by human ears and which I could never have played on my own. In the music were the conversations between Eagles and flowers, between dust and breeze, between dew and toiling insects, between the moon and the sun. The eagles above stopped, suspended in air, the cool breeze wrapped itself around me and squirrels and birds sat around me, listening to this music, ignoring me completely.

I too listened, assured of my irrelevance but happy in it.

After many hours, the final notes dripped from my Oud and finally stopped. Silence cloaked the mountains and the only sound was of me breathing.

I placed the Oud with great respect under a tree. A tender green leaf drifted down on it.

I turned and walked slowly down the mountain. Towards Jizan.

✦ ✦ ✦

30

Poems in Sand

by Sami al-Mutlaq[2]

Bismillah ar-Rahman ar-Rahim

What are we but mere drifting sand in the vast desert of time and space? Who shall tell me why we are born, who we are to serve and to whom we shall reveal love?

I have traveled in the Rub al-Khali, and where people have seen emptiness, I have seen the ghosts of children playing with the dreams of those long departed, whose skeletons have become sand. I have seen men walk alone in a silent caravan, with no real destiny except perhaps the silent welcome of a lonely wife, who was now quiet as the winds on which the eagles soar. With them, their camels have walked, contemptuous of existence, their wooden bells ringing out in the dead of night,

2 a pseudonym used by the author

reminding the ghosts watching from behind dunes, that they are not intruders, but vehicles for the tormented ambitions of weak men.

Many years ago, I cloaked my face and began one such journey, unannounced, as was my custom, but only after invoking the blessings of those who seek only to love. Love would surround me as a slowly whirling cloak, and protect me from the cruel hot winds of the Rub al-Khali. I held the hand of kind wishes and set out to Shibam. I carried dates and incense as a courier for another man, who envied me my permanent longing for solitude. I traveled from Tabuk in the far north to Shibam in Yemen. During the day, I walked. At night, I walked too, for the moon and stars shone in the clear sky and asked me not to rest but to understand eternal beauty and the true benediction of Allah.

Two days from the town of Qatif, as the sun sank in a pool of red, I came across three men, resting with their camels. We greeted each other solemnly and I inquired if I might rest nearby as well. They insisted that I share their food and we exchanged stories and searched for common acquaintances. We were surprised that the names of people in familiar towns were not familiar to either of us. I inquired about al-Qahtani of Tabuk but they knew not of him, though they said their family was from Tabuk. They inquired if I knew of al-Idris from Buraydah, but I did not know of him even though I had spent many waking moments there.

The stars shone in great brilliance that night. The camels looked at each other with half-closed eyes. One of the men took out an Oud and played. The tunes were created then, stroked by starlight, and ravished the nearby sands without touching them. The night winds calmed down and stopped to listen. The others sang, asking from Allah that fellow-men know of love and loneliness, and that music bring rest to the troubled mind. Such was the gentleness in their music. I listened, with my head resting against the side of my camel, and his heart and mine came together, to the beat of the dark night. I wrote poems in the sand, with words I had not heard of before. And I saw the sand embrace them and take them down, down, down, to the hearts of poets who were lost for so many years in the desert. The men sang my poems, and the words now crept over the dunes and slipped away into the night. I slept, dreamlessly. But no, there was light. The light of love from ghosts who had listened to the music and held it in their hands.

When I awoke, it was the dawn and the men had gone. For the first time, I saw the tracks of camels leading away, and the sand not erasing them. From the far distance, I heard the Oud and I knew that I was not to go towards the music.

I walked towards Shibam, alone, with the bells of my camel, subdued, but caressing, now with the fragrance of love.